from this moment

KATRINA MARIE

Editor: Small Edits

Cover Design: Aurora Hale

To Hubs for giving me my happily ever after.

MY PALMS ARE SWEATY, and I wipe them on my jeans to dry them off. It doesn't help. Now my jeans have sweat streaks. This is not going how I planned. It's insanely hot today, and the arboretum is teeming with people. I should have picked a weekday to visit, but Tonya has been busy helping her mom at the real estate office, and my mom can't take off during the week. I couldn't do this without them here.

Tonya is pushing the stroller ahead of me, taking her time looking at all the flowers and plants that grow here. It's beautiful and the perfect setting for the question I want to ask her. We are halfway through the gardens when we come to a beautiful waterfall. There are trees surrounding a small man-made pool. A brick ledge separates us from the water, but there is an expanse of lawn right in front. "This looks like a good place to have lunch."

"Sounds good," Tonya chirps as she unbuckles Layla from the stroller. "There's a tree right over there that would be perfect for the shade."

The wagon I've been pulling behind me is about to get a little bit lighter, at least. The main reason we brought it is to carry the picnic lunch we made at Tonya's this morning. It was a great investment, and I can see us getting years of use out of it as Layla gets older. I pull the light blanket out and spread it across the green grass. While I get the food out, Tonya gets Layla set up with her tummy time mat. She's not ready for the sandwiches we have packed, but I packed bottled water and the formula I keep at my house. I can't wait until she hits those milestones when she can eat and run around. She's not much younger than my nephew, and I have a blast with that kid.

I never imagined I would have a family at such a young age. But I'm grateful for the day Tonya fought me over that art project. It gave me a chance to get to know her, and fall in love with her. Pregnant and all. I wouldn't take back the last seven months for anything. These two ladies complete me in a way I don't completely understand, but I plan on making that permanent.

Layla is cooing on her mat, tiny fists reaching into the air trying to grab the toys hanging above her. Tonya's chatting with my mom about baby stuff as usual. I don't think anyone besides Tonya's parents are as happy to be in Layla's life as my mom is. Ok, well, maybe Cami. Having her best friend live with her is the best thing ever.

She's the one who helped me plan this excursion. I'm shocked she's kept it quiet this long. She doesn't keep any secrets from Tonya. At least, not anymore. Since she's stepped away from her crazy ass parents, she's been a lot more open with Tonya. It's definitely a good thing, because my girl was worried about her bestie all the time.

I'm so busy watching the amazing relationship she has with my mom that I don't hear Mrs. Burgess talking. "I'm sorry, what?"

She leans in and whispers, "Are you ready?" Nodding her head at Tonya a big grin takes over her face.

Of course, she knows, I did things the old-fashioned way and asked Mr. Burgess for his blessing. He still had his reservations. Mostly because he didn't believe my intentions were pure when it came to dating his daughter. But he sees how in love I am with Tonya. He knows there's nothing that could turn me away from her. He may have also been impressed when I stood up to Jake that one time in their yard. But that's a whole other story. One I'm working on being okay with. Him being a part of Layla's life isn't my decision, but I'm glad he's finally stepping up to the plate. It'll be better for her if she has all parents on the same page.

I shake thoughts of Tonya's ex away. Nodding at Mrs. Burgess, I try to grab Tonya's attention. "Can y'all watch the princess while Tonya and I take a walk?"

"Absolutely," both of our moms say at the same time. I can see how hard it is for them to hide their excitement, so I hold out my hand to Tonya before they give everything away.

She grabs it, happy to get some us time for a little bit. Even if it is for a short walk. She tries not to ask her parents to babysit too often. In her eyes, she's the one who had Layla, so she's her responsibility. Her parents try nudging her to just leave her with them, but she doesn't always give in. Their reasoning... "she still needs to go out and live." I agree with them completely, but Tonya can be stubborn.

I double check my pocket to ensure the ring is there before we walk off. Getting down on one knee without the ring would be pretty damn embarrassing. My hands are sweating again and I'm worried she'll pick up on how nervous I am. Maybe she'll just think it's the heat, and not say anything.

"Thank you for bringing us out here today." She leans into me, pulling her hand from mine, and wrapping her arm around my waist.

A part of me wants to pull away because it's hot and I don't want to get sweat all over her, but I quiet that thought. Instead, I pull her closer, reveling in the fact that she's all mine. "Absolutely. Flowers aren't really my thing, but I knew it would make you and our moms happy. Besides, we can get some adorable pictures of Layla with all the bright colors."

She smacks her forehead. "I didn't even think of that. We've wasted all this time with the first half of the gardens." Shaking her head, she continues, "Now, I feel like we need to go back so we can get pictures."

"I'm sure there are plenty of flowers in the remaining gardens." I chuckle. She gets so worked up about the tiniest things. It would annoy some people, but I think it's adorable.

"You're right." She gives me a quick side hug and we continue walking.

"I wonder if there are any fish in that pond," I muse. I'm trying to find a reason to get her over there. We need the perfect backdrop. Mom and Mrs. Burgess are slowly getting closer to where we're standing. Layla pulling my mom's hair. "Look, I think I saw something ripple the water." I need her to not pay attention to our moms.

As she leans over the brick wall, I use the distraction to dig the ring out of my pocket. I should have put it in a pouch or something. Small pieces of lint hang off it, and I do my best to pull them all out before she turns back around.

"Reaf," she says, still eyeing the pond. "I don't see any-" Her words die on her lips when she notices I'm no longer standing beside her, but down on one knee.

"Tonya." Her name is stuck in my throat. Now is not the time to be nervous. Gah, I sound like a teenager whose voice is still cracking. Clearing my throat, I hope there are no more mishaps. "I know we haven't been together for very long, but what I *do* know is that I want you in my life every day for years to come. I want to wake up to your beautiful face every morning, and shower you with the love you deserve."

"What the hell are you doing, Reaf?" She whispers, frantically. Good, I've caught her off guard. She had no idea this was going to happen. Score one for all the people who kept it quiet.

I shrug, and watch her nose scrunch up at the simple gesture. "Um, I'm trying to propose to you if you'll let me finish." She waves her hand, wanting me to continue. "Where was I? Oh yeah, I want to shower you with love. I want to be the person you lean on when you're having a bad day, and the one who celebrates all the successes you have along the way. And, one day I'd love to have babies with you, and grow our family." She snorts at that. "Will you marry me?"

She doesn't say anything. She stares at me, and then looks at our moms watching on the sidelines with their phones out. Shit. I've done the wrong thing. She's not ready for this, and I screwed everything up. "I'm sorry, it's too early to profess my undying love for you." I begin tucking the ring back into my pocket.

Tonya's hand whips out grabbing mine before I can put it back, almost knocking the ring out of my hand. "Why are you putting it away? I never answered."

"Which is why I assumed the answer would be no."

"You know what happens when you assume, right?" She smirks. That's a good thing...I think.

"Yeah, yeah. It makes an ass out of you and me." I grab her hand with my free one. "So, are you going to answer?" I hate the uncertainty in the question. But I fear rejection even more.

She pulls the hand not entwined with mine back, and taps her chin. "I don't know," she answers. "Does this include you also cooking breakfast and pretty much most other meals? Because we both know I can't even boil water without burning the pan."

"That's because you forget about it." A grin spreads across my face. She's going to say yes, I just know it. "And, yes I'll cook anytime you ask. Or, you know, order take out if I don't feel like it."

"Then YES," she shouts, throwing her arms around my neck, nearly knocking me over. She kisses my cheeks, chin, lips. Anywhere she can reach. Whispering in my ear, she says, "The promise of cooking won me over." She pulls back and winks. "Now, can I see the ring?"

I almost forgot about it. I grab her hand, and slowly slide the ring on her finger. Tears well up in my eyes and almost spill over. She's just made me the happiest guy on the planet. Our moms are clapping and yelling their congratulations while people look at us curiously. When they see what's happening, another roar of applause is heard. I lean Tonya back, and kiss her long and deep. They need to see just how in love with this woman I am.

"I'm getting married," Tonya yells into the hot summer air.

I can't help but be amazed at her beauty. Not just in her looks, but her love of her child and how much she cares about others in general. "I love you," I murmur into her ear.

"I love you, too. You make me happier than anyone in this world." She glances at Layla. "Except for maybe her."

I place a chaste kiss on her lips. "I plan on making you happy for the rest of our lives."

tonya

WHAT WAS I thinking when I decided to plan a wedding while working and still going to school? At any point someone could have said, "Maybe you should wait until the summer when you have more time." But they didn't. Not one person in my family, or group of friends, told me to hold off.

I'm not entirely sure I would have listened anyway. The only reason I've been so adamant to have it in the Spring is because I don't want my great-grandmother to endure any sort of heat if she doesn't have to. I know she would have done it because she loves me, but why make her suffer. Hell, why make anyone suffer. It gets hot in Texas, and while the ceremony will be inside, the after-party won't be.

To be honest, I'm freaking out. The wedding is in two weeks, and there is still so much left to do. The dresses need to be fitted for everyone, and there are so many decorations that need to be made. There aren't enough hours in the day to get it all done unless I take off from work.

Everything would be so much easier if Cami and Darcy were here. But no…They are hundreds of miles away studying for their midterms, which I also need to do. They will be here in a week, and they better be ready to work. There will be a lot of last-minute crafting and everything else.

"What are you doing, sweetie?" I've been so absorbed in my thoughts that I don't hear my mom walk up behind me.

"Contemplating running off to Vegas, and eloping." I deadpan. There's a piece of paper with a massive check-list sitting in front of me, what else would I be doing?

"You don't mean that." She pulls out the chair next to me and sits down. "You would break Lala's heart if you did."

I saw that guilt trip coming from a mile away. "I know. There's just so much to do, and I'm running out of time." I pull the blanket draped over my legs a little tighter. Even though it's the beginning of March, we are having a weird cold snap. I blame it on the freak ice storm we had back at Christmas. It threw everything off, and the weather has been from one extreme to the other. "What if it doesn't warm up by the time the wedding gets here? We don't have a backup plan for the reception."

"Don't worry about the weather." Mom soothes. I

know she's trying to get me to calm down, but it feels like she's pushing my concerns aside. "You can't control what Mother Nature does. We'll come up with a plan in case it's cold." She grabs the list from in front of me, scanning the hastily scribbled mess. I wanted to get an idea of everything that needs to get done, and it turned into a brain dump. I wouldn't be surprised if random points from studying ended up on it. At this point, anything is possible. "Why don't you delegate some of this to the girls? I mean, I can help. But I also know they want to help. They don't want you so stressed out."

"I can't ask for their help. They are busy with studying." Sighing, I rest my head on top of the kitchen table. "I don't want to be the reason they do badly on their exams."

Mom's chair scoots back from the counter and a few seconds later I hear the hum of the microwave. What is she doing? I close my eyes, debating whether I should try to get stuff done, or take a nap right where I am. Normally the thought wouldn't even cross my mind, but Layla is with Jake and Charleigh for a few hours, and I could definitely use the rest. I have a feeling I will be depending on him more and more until the wedding.

A minute after the microwave dings, Mom is back at the kitchen table sliding a plate across the mostly smooth surface. Peeking through the strands of my hair, I see the plate with a large brownie that looks delicious. "I can't eat that." I sit up and shake my head. "If I eat everything you keep shoving my way, I'll never fit into my dress."

"One little brownie isn't going to kill you," she snaps.

"That," I point to the brownie in question. "Is not little. It's almost as big as the plate."

"It's a small plate. There's no need for exaggeration."

"Fine, I'll eat the brownie." I grumble.

"Good." She nods, victorious. "Why don't you ask Caroline to help? She's one of your bridesmaids, too, you know?"

"I don't know." I shove a forkful of the gooey chocolate goodness into my mouth. "I'll feel bad pulling her away from David. She works so much and rarely gets to see him as it is."

"She's going to be your sister-in-law, and I know for a fact she'd be happy to help." She sticks her own fork into the brownie. I almost pull the plate closer to me so I don't have to share, but decide against it. I think she's just as stressed as I am. Work has been crazy busy, and she's gotten home late every night for the past couple of weeks. "And, you wouldn't be taking her away from David. He could come over with her. If anything, he'll be able to chase Layla around the house and keep her out of trouble."

I snort. "More like destroy everything. For such a cute kid, he can destroy a play area in two seconds flat." I would know. I've seen him do it many times.

"We'll clean it up after if they make a mess." She takes a bite of the brownie and places her fork on the plate. "I know you're trying to do it all on your own, but you have people around you that want to help." She pats my back, reassuringly. "I'm sure even Reaf would risk a few burns from the glue gun to help with whatever decorations need to be made."

A giggle bubbles up from inside me. "That would actually be pretty hysterical." And it would be. Seeing this manly man wield a hot glue gun. I laugh and almost choke. "I can picture it now."

Mom rolls her eyes. "It's not that funny, but I see your point." Sliding the chair back once more, she looks at me. "Please call Caroline. I know you have a lot on your plate, but let some of us ease the burden." Then she walks out. I guess she had nothing else to say.

I pull my cell phone from the other side of the table.

Me: Hey, future sis. Can you come over?

Caroline: I thought you'd never ask. ;) Be there in twenty.

It's time to start taking more of my mom's words of wisdom.

* * *

The sun is shining brightly through my window, and I want nothing more than to pull the covers over my head and go back to sleep. But... I can't. I have to work, study, take care of little Miss Layla.

Even with Caroline's help, I still have so much to do. Her coming to my rescue last night relieved some of the stress I've been feeling. But there's still so much on my plate that I feel like I'm drowning. Reaf tagged along with her to see what he could do to help. Unfortunately, there wasn't much he could do. He spent most of the evening making sure David didn't break anything. And, making sure Layla didn't climb onto anything.

I throw the blanket off of me, and mentally run through everything I have to accomplish today. One, work until twelve. Two, go to class and study until six. Three, pick up Layla from daycare. For, text Cami and Darcy to see when they will be in this weekend. Five, cook dinner, play with Layla, and get her tucked into bed. Six, sleep. I've been ticking off my fingers as I think of each thing that needs to be done only to realize there isn't another finger to tick off for sleep. Ah well, I'll fit it in there somewhere.

Rolling over, I grab my phone from the nightstand. There's no sense in letting the alarm go off when I'm already awake. Besides, the loud blaring will no doubt wake up everyone in the house, especially Layla. That little girl is my reason for breathing, but she has become a handful since she started walking. I can't keep that child out of anything.

I open the text app to knock out some of my to do list before I get ready for work. The oncoming days will be filled to the brim, and I need my support system to get me through it. Chocolate would also help.

Tonya: When are you guys coming home?

Cami: As soon as we are done with finals, we will be headed that way. So, we'll be there late Thursday afternoon.

Tonya: Sounds good! I'll see you then. Good luck on your finals!

Cami: You too, girl.

There's one conversation out of the way. Now, to text Jake.

Tonya: How do you feel about more father daughter time?

Jake: I feel like that's a question you shouldn't even have to ask. Why? What's up?

. . .

Tonya: Do you think you or Charleigh could pick Layla up from daycare tomorrow? I have a dress fitting appointment.

Jake: Sure thing. One of us will be there to get her.

Tonya: Thanks.

I hate having to rely on them as much as I have needed to these past few weeks. Not because he's a bad dad or anything, but we are still trying to figure out how to effectively co-parent. We have it down for the most part, it just needs a little fine tuning. I feel like I'm taking advantage of them sometimes. Jake and Charleigh deny it whenever I ask them for help. But I can't help feeling that way since I've been the only one responsible for her until recently. It's hard letting go of that little bit of control, especially since I've been feeling so out of control and overwhelmed lately.

There's a rustling coming through the baby monitor, and I nearly jump off the bed. Shit, that stupid monitor scares me every single time a noise comes from her room. I can hear her singing to herself which means she's up and ready to see what trouble she can get into today. I'm sure it's lots. So much for taking a shower before she woke up. I guess we'll be taking one together. One handed showers are not the easiest thing in the world, but it's bonding time I cherish. We get so little time together with work and school. I know I'll miss these days when she's older.

Pausing outside her doorway, I listen to her sweet voice as she mumbles to herself. She gave me hell the first few months of her life, but these small moments are worth it all. "Hey baby, girl," I whisper as I step into her room.

The smile that spreads across her face is enough to melt anyone's heart. She grabs the railing of the crib, bouncing up and down. "Mama." I could have jumped for joy when my name spilled from her lips the first time. My mom refused to believe it is was her first word. She was secretly hoping it would be Gram. For the life of me I can't figure out why she picked that name for Layla to call her. To each their own, I guess.

"Want to go take a shower with Mommy?" Her grabby hands are all the affirmation I need. "First, let's get you out of this stinking diaper."

Once she's free of her clothes, and the diaper, I walk us to the bathroom. She sits on the rug, playing with the bathtub toys I keep in there for her. A quick shower is what we both need to conquer the day. At least, that's what I hope.

Once we're dressed and fed, I load her into her car seat. Hopefully, I can make it through this day with my sanity intact.

TWO

reaf

THE FACT that I get to marry the person I love most in just under two weeks is the only thing that is keeping me going today at the shop. So many cars have come through the garage today. Families getting ready for road trips with their kids, and college students making sure all is okay before they head to the coast for Spring Break.

Truth be told, I've always been a little envious of those that can go do all these things during their breaks from school. I've always worked to help my mom as much as possible. It wasn't easy after my dad left. Bryce doesn't even remember him. On the days I'm feeling jealous, I just think of all the stupid things I won't get caught doing, and how my family always has each other's back.

A small part of me wonders if Tonya wishes she could join in the shenanigans included during most Spring Break trips. But the other part doesn't care because soon

I'll be her other half and we make our own traditions and plans.

"Reaf," my boss calls across the garage. "Check on the customer that just walked in. After you get done with whatever they need, you can leave for the day."

"Sure thing." My hands are almost black from the oil change I just finished. I grab the closest towel while walking to the side door that leads into the lobby area. It's nice to get a little fresh air, even if it's from inside the building. I take a deep breath, grateful for the break from the smell of gas, oil and tools.

Throwing the shop towel into the nearby trash can, I don't look up as I ask, "How can I help you today?"

"For starters, you can call off your wedding to Tonya. She's the only real shot my son has at a normal life, instead of being with that girl that works in the tattoo shop." A female voice says, full of venom.

Why in the hell is Jake's mom here? And what the actual fuck? Who starts a conversation like that? "Excuse me?" I'm so taken aback that I don't have any other words.

"You heard me." She straightens to her full height and looks down her nose at me. To her I'm nobody. Not worth the dirt on the bottom of her shiny, low heels. "Call off your wedding, and give Jake the chance to be with the mother of his child."

"I'm sorry, ma'am, but that's not going to happen. Jake doesn't want anything to do with you, or your husband. And he's perfectly happy with Charleigh. You can't order me to do your bidding. I'm in love with Tonya and I'll be making her my wife next weekend." I roll up the sleeves of my long sleeve shirt. "Now, if you don't have a car you wish to be serviced, I suggest you vacate the premises."

The glare she shoots me is enough to make a weaker man bow down to her demands. But I've dealt with people like her my entire life. I've never let others push me around, and I'm sure as hell not going to let her do it. She huffs when she sees I'm not going to give and turns to leave. Before she walks out the door, she makes a parting statement. "This isn't over."

Once she's out of sight, I let out a sigh of relief. What the hell gives her the right to ask me to do something like that. I'm not worried about Tonya's feelings for me, but I'd be lying if I said the interaction didn't rankle.

"Who was that?" Rick, my boss, asks as he walks into the lobby.

"Just a bitter old woman trying to cause problems." I glance into the now mostly empty garage. "Can I head out now?"

He nods and looks at the calendar for tomorrow. "Try to be in early tomorrow. It's going to be another busy one."

"Okay." I don't give him a chance to say anything else. I grab my keys from the drawer under the counter and hurry out the door. I really need to see my girl right now.

* * *

The drive to Tonya's house goes by in a blur. I can't believe the audacity of Jake's mom. Did she really think I was going to roll over and let her dictate what I'm going to do? She must be out of her damn mind to even entertain the idea.

I check the review mirror, more out of habit than anything else, and I'm surprised my face isn't flushed with anger. I need to get my emotions under control before I get there. I don't want her to see how pissed off I am.

Do I even tell her? She's already stressed with all the wedding planning. I don't want to add this to her already full plate. If she won't let me help with decorations, or anything else for that matter, the least I can do is keep this away from her.

I park the car and take a few deep breaths, doing everything I can to rein in my frustration. Minutes later, I'm at the front door and knocking on the solid wood. A spring inspired wreath hangs in the middle, and almost falls down when I knock again. That's weird. She's usually home by now. I didn't even bother to look in the driveway to see if her car was here.

Just as I turn around, the door swings open. "Reaf, what are you doing here?" Mr. Burgess's booming voice comes from the doorway.

"I came by to see Tonya, and ask if she needed me to do anything." It's not a complete lie. I did come by to see her. But I know she won't let me do anything to help her. She's so freaking stubborn it's unreal. I'm confident she gets it from her dad.

"She's not here right now." He opens the door wider. "You can come in, though. She should be here soon."

I glance longingly at my car. It's nothing personal against her dad, but spending time with him without Tonya as a buffer is always awkward. He wasn't the biggest fan of me when I first started dating his daughter over a year ago. Yes, he gave me his blessing, and I'm sure the only reason is because he sees how happy I make her. Or, that she's so stubborn that she would have run off with me. It could go either way.

I face him, and begin toward the door. "Thanks, Mr. Burgess." Shutting the door softly behind me, I follow him into the living room. "Where is she anyway?"

He takes a seat on the couch facing the television. There's a college basketball game showing on the screen with the volume muted. "Reaf, you'll be family soon. How many times do I have to tell you to call me Jason?"

"Sorry, sir." I mumble. "It's just weird calling y'all by your first names. Blame that on my mom."

"Maggie did a fine job of raising you." Grabbing his drink off the end table, he sinks back into the sofa. "Tonya's at her dress fitting. It was the only time she could fit in this week before going again when the rest of girls are with her." He nods to the space on the other side of the couch. "Watch the game with me."

I take a closer look at the television before sitting down. "Is that Hilltown U?"

"Yep. That guy Darcy brought with her over Christmas break plays for the team. I figured I'd check him out and see if he's any good."

"Is he?"

"Yeah. The kid's decent considering he had a late start."

I sit back against the couch, watching Derrick run from one side of the court to the other. Jason isn't wrong, he's pretty good. His spot on the team is definitely well deserved. He didn't say much when they were here. He spent most of the time following Darcy around like a puppy or listening to the rest of us guys talk while the girls were planning the wedding. It'd be great to get to know him a little better since he's friends with Travis, and the two of us have gotten to be good friends.

Lost in the sound of shoes squeaking and the ball being dribbled, I almost don't notice the silence in the house. There should be the sound of annoying toys being played with. "Where's Layla?"

"With her dad," Jason grunts.

"Why?" I'm not upset that she's with Jake. Well...not completely. She could have called me and had me pick her up to help her out. I don't understand why she has to be so damn stubborn.

"She says it's so Layla has more time to bond with Jake. But I don't know. She's never been one to rely on anyone else, least of all him."

"Speaking of," I throw out into the silence.

"If it's something bad about Jake I don't want to know. He's come a long way since he moved back, and as much as it kills me to say it, I think him being with Layla as much as possible is a good thing."

I can't even argue with him because it's true. He's done a complete one-eighty from the jealous asshole that was pestering Tonya over a year ago. Him and Charleigh are perfect for each other, and I'm happy we all get along. I wish Caroline and her ex could be like that for David. But that's next to impossible.

Taking a deep breath, I let it out slowly. "It's not about Jake per se, but it is about his mother."

"What the hell is Diane up to now?" He quickly stands. "Hold on to that thought, I'm going to grab a beer. I have a feeling I'll need it for this."

I nod at his retreating back. Hell, I need drink for this. Her insanity is what had me hauling ass over here to see me girl. Instead I get to hang out with her dad. It's not a bad thing. I just feel weird being here without her.

Sitting down in his spot, Jason takes a long sip from the amber bottle. He may need something stronger than that. "Okay, tell me what the great Diane was up to today."

I rub my hand over my face, wishing I didn't have to have this conversation at all, but I have to. Maybe he can tell me whether I should inform Tonya. "She came into the shop today and basically demanded I call off the wedding."

"Why would you do that?"

"In her words…because I'm not worthy and Jake is Layla's father. They should be together to make the perfect little family." I really wish he would have offered me one of those beers. I could use one right now, that's for sure.

"She's so full of shit," Jason barks. I jump back in surprise, trying to think of time I've heard him cuss, and I can't come up with one. "She only wants them to look like a cookie cutter family so they can save face." He gives me a stern look. "You know that, right?"

"Yeah," I breathe out. "But it really ticked me off. I told her if she didn't need her car serviced, she needed to leave the premises."

His eyes widened in surprise. "Are you serious? What did she do?"

"She looked at me like she couldn't believe I had the audacity to stand up to her."

"That sounds about right," he shakes his head. "You aren't going to tell Tonya, are you?"

"I was hoping you would lead me in the direction I need to take with her."

He squeezes the bridge of his nose between his thumb and forefinger as if he's fighting off an oncoming headache. "I wouldn't tell her. She's already freaking out about everything she needs to get done, and this would only be one more thing to stress her out."

I nod and turn back to the game. "Thanks, that's what I was thinking as well."

"I'm glad you opened up to me, Reaf."

He begins watching the game again, as if we didn't just agree to share a secret between us. I wish I knew what I could do to help ease Tonya's burden, but any time I ask, she waves me off. I know this would stress her out even more, and it's a wise choice not to tell her. But, if she finds out, she's going to be so pissed.

tonya

TEARS THREATEN to spill from my eyes. The dress fitting did not go the way I planned. A small part of me wishes I would have waited until Cami and Darcy were here to go with me. But...that wouldn't have given the store enough time for alterations.

The sound of birds chirping merrily in the cool spring air does nothing to improve my mood, and I rush to my car to get some peace before I go home. Sliding on to the driver seat, I put my key in the ignition, but don't turn it. Instead, I slump forward until my forehead rests on the steering wheel.

The dress didn't fit. I wish I could say it's because it needed to be taken in, but I could barely zip the damn thing up. No matter how much I tried to suck in, the stupid zipper wouldn't budge. It took everything in me not to sit in the middle of the bridal store and bawl my eyes out. The only thing that kept me from doing it is the sympathetic look in the sales person's eyes. I would not let her see how much it bothered me.

Resigned, I start the car and pull out of the parking lot. It's going to be salads and healthy foods until my wedding day, no matter how magnificent the food Mom cooks smells. The woman has got to stop shoving brownies and all the other sweets she bakes at me. And, I need to be strong enough to stop accepting them. I know it's her way of showing me she cares, but it's put an unfortunate kink in everything. I'm only happy I found out now instead of next week when the girls come in.

The drive home is somber. I don't even bother turning the radio on, insisting in wallowing in my frustration. I pass families playing in their front yards without a care in the world. I would have much rather been home with Layla, chasing her around the house. But she won't be home for another hour. Jake really stepped up when I asked him to watch Layla for me, even offering to bring her home instead of me driving to Dallas to pick her up. It only makes me realize how great Charleigh is for him. She grounds him in a way I never did, and it shows.

Reaf's car is in front of the house when I pull into the driveway, and I wonder how long he's been here. I glance in the mirror as soon as I put the car in park, only now noticing the single, solitary tear sliding down my cheek. I need to get my shit together before I walk inside. I don't want him to see how stressed and emotional I am right now.

Wiping the tear from my face, I put on the biggest smile I can muster, which isn't very big at all. Geez, I can't even make this wedding happen without any issues. How am I going to manage a family when we're on our own in a couple of weeks? It hasn't been difficult so far because Layla and I live with my parents while Reaf lives with his mom and siblings. But it's going to be a whole new adjustment when we move into the small apartment we have waiting for us.

I don't have time to think about that right now, though. I square my shoulders and grab my bag before opening the car door. I will put on a brave face even though self-doubt is eating away at me.

Squeaking sneakers and whistles come from the television in the living room when I open the door. Dad must have roped him into watching a game with him while he was waiting on me. I put my bag on the table in the entry way and round the corner. I was right. The both of them are sitting on the edge of their seats as they watch Hilltown University play. I wasn't sure Dad would ever truly accept Reaf. After my fiasco of a relationship with Jake, he remains cautious. Waiting to swoop in to rescue me should the need arise. But that is one thing I'm certain won't happen with Reaf. My dad will never have a reason to intervene in our relationship. I think he knows that, even if he won't admit it.

They didn't even look up when I walked in. Their attention solely on the game being played on TV. "Hey guys, whatcha doing?" I rock slowly from heel to toe, waiting to see who is going to respond first.

"You're home," Reaf exclaims and jumps up from the couch.

"Obviously," I snort. "Otherwise we'd have a bigger issue with doppelgängers."

"You're such a nerd," he protests. "Come watch the last few minutes of the game with us." He motions to the couch he's standing in front of. "Derrick's team is playing and they are tied."

I take a seat between him and my father, watching the basketball players run from one end of the court to the other, doing their best to block shots. "Has it been a good game?"

Reaf points to himself then the TV. "You know I don't typically watch basketball, but I haven't been able to pull my eyes from the screen. Derrick has some skills on the court."

Laughter is the only response I can give him because it's true. I haven't seen him watch anything relating to sports. "What do you think of Darcy's boyfriend, Dad?"

"He's pretty good" he grunts. "How was the dress fitting?"

I close my eyes and count to three not wanting to get into the disaster it was. Before I have a chance to answer, Dad abruptly stands. "Shoot," he yells at the TV as if the players can actually hear him. That's the one thing I never understood about watching sports. What's the point of yelling at a screen? It's not going to change anything.

I look up, and see that Derrick has the ball. There are seconds left of the game. He takes a deep breath and the ball leaves his hands. Soaring through the air until it slides into the hoop. It's a good thing Layla isn't here; their cheering would only have her joining in. If for no other reason than to hear her own voice. Ugh, this is why I don't do sports. It's a whole bunch of loud noise in one tiny space.

"Where's Layla?" Dad asks as he picks up his bottle of beer from the end table.

"Jake is bringing her home soon," I shrug. Grateful for the tiny break in adulting. Don't get me wrong, I love my daughter fiercely. But...it's also nice to have a little bit of time all to myself.

"Well," Dad begins walking toward the kitchen. "I'll let y'all have some space. I need to get ready for work tomorrow anyway."

"Thanks," I smile.

Reaf pulls me into his arms, and I relax into him. Feeling the disaster of the dress fitting melt away as I sink further into his embrace. As stressful as planning has been, I don't regret any of it. In the end, Reaf will be mine and I will be his. He's my home, and I couldn't ask for a better partner in life.

He places a kiss on the top of my head. "I take it the fitting didn't go well."

"That would be an understatement," I sigh. "But it's

okay because it will be fixed by the time I go back with the girls."

"That's good." His hand trails up and down my arm, leaving goosebumps on my skin. I was worried that feeling would fade, but it only grows stronger. Most days, anyway. There are some days where I want to throw out the wedding plans and say to hell with it. Eloping would be so much easier.

The doorbell rings, signaling the arrival of my sweet girl. Reaf doesn't let me answer the door. Sliding out from under me he places a pillow in the spot he just vacated, and goes to answer the door.

"Mama, mama, mama." I hear Layla calling me repeatedly. I can't stop the small smile from forming on my lips and get up to meet them at the door.

"Hi, Baby Girl," I grab her under her outstretched arms. "Did you miss me?"

Her only response is to grab my face and kiss me. That puddle on the floor would be my heart melting from her sweetness.

"Hey, Tonya," Charleigh chirps from beside Jake. "How are you?"

"Good," I shrug. "Well, as good as I can be trying to balance everything."

"I don't know how you do it. That girl," she points at Layla. "Wears me out every time we have her. She's constantly waddling around and getting into everything she can reach. She even tries to get the stuff she can't reach. Where does she get her energy from?"

Shaking my head, I laugh. "I have no idea, but I wish I could bottle it up and use it to get through my days."

"I don't blame you."

Jake leans in to give Layla a quick kiss on the back of her head. "Bye, Sweetheart. I'll see you later."

"Bye, bye," The two words fall from her tiny lips as she snuggles into me.

Jake turns to me, "We've already fed her, so she should be good to go to bed. If you need us to keep her more over the next week, let me know. We'll take her whenever you need us to so y'all can get things done."

"Thanks, Jake." I move Layla to my hip and lean into Reaf. "We might take you up on that."

"I mean it, any time. I love spending time with her. Even if the house looks like a tornado hit it when she leaves."

"I'll text you and let you know if we need you."

"Bye," they wave and walk to their car.

Reaf swoops Layla out of my arms. "I will put her to bed." He turns my body back toward the living room and couch. "You go lie back down. I'll see what your mom has stowed away in the fridge once she's asleep."

"You don't have to-" I begin, but he cuts me off.

"I know I don't have to do it. I want to. I know all of this has been rough on you with everything else, and I want to help."

"Thank you," I whisper.

He places a finger under my chin and lifts it until my eyes meet his. "You're welcome. But I'm here for the long haul. Otherwise I wouldn't have asked you to marry me." He pauses for a second. "I want to help you. I want to ease your burdens. But I can't do that if you are always so damn stubborn."

Grinning, I place a quick kiss on his lips. "I'll try to be less stubborn, but I make no promises."

Reaf walks with Layla to her room, and I pull the blanket off the back of the couch and lie down. I can faintly hear him softly humming to her as he puts her to sleep. I let the sound of his voice calm me. She's not the only one that falls asleep to the sound of his voice. Before long, my eyes close and I fall asleep on the couch knowing how lucky I truly am.

"Oh my gosh," Cami exclaims. "It feels like it's been forever since I've seen you." She throws her arms around me, pulling me into a hug. The crazy woman didn't even knock. Not that she has to since she has a key. But a little warning would have been nice. I could have been naked or something.

"It's literally been a month and a half," I deadpan. She has entirely too much energy. Did she stop at every coffee shop between Hilltown and Asheville?

"That's still too long." The suitcase by her feet falls over when she bumps into it. Bending down, she grabs the handle and wheels it into my bedroom. Right in the middle of the floor. I see her tidiness hasn't improved.

Pushing the suitcase to the side, I make room for Darcy to come into my room. She hasn't reached the same level of comfort in my home that Cami has. "You can set your stuff wherever you want." I whirl around on Cami. "And, you. Keep it down. You're going to wake Layla up."

She practically runs toward the door. "I have to go see my baby girl."

I step in front of her, blocking her path. "If you wake that child up... I. Will. Cut. You."

"With what? Your bitchiness?" She rolls her eyes. "Sorry, sister. Your threats don't scare me." She sucks in a big breath. "But I will leave her alone. Not because of you, just so you know. We need to catch up on what needs to be done, and everything else."

"Tell me again why I call you my best friend?"

"Every gal needs a witty BFF. You lucked out and have two." She flops onto my bed, hair splayed across the comforter.

Darcy snorts, "Don't bring me into this. I'm witty, but I'm not loud."

Cami tries to shrug but she doesn't have any traction on the fabric. I laugh, she's ridiculous but I wouldn't have her any other way. She's loud, brash, and a hot mess on the best of days. She always has my back and isn't scared to defend those she loves.

"So," Cami calls out. "What do you need us to do? Give me directions."

Darcy sits on the end of the bed and I crawl onto the

space between them. "Not much right now. Caroline helped me with the decorations earlier this week. We have dress fittings in a few hours, but we're free until then."

"Let's go watch a movie or somethings." Cami says. "I've been holed up in the library all week studying for exams. I need something to calm my mind."

We file out of the room and make ourselves comfortable on the couch. At least until I remember that I still need to start the movie. Instead, I grab the remote and scroll through what's playing on the TV. It's definitely lazy, but I'm okay with that. This week has been hectic and I only want a few moments of peace. I don't want to worry about school, work, or burn the hell out of myself with the hot glue gun. They really should put warnings on those things for adults. It's just not safe.

I've zoned out while flipping through the options, and the sound of Cami's voice breaking the silence makes me jump. "Look, a Harry Potter marathon. I haven't watched that in ages."

I press select, and toss the remote on the table, flinching at the loud thump it makes. I take a moment to listen. Trying to determine if the noise woke Layla up. Luckily, I don't hear anything coming from her room. I grab the baby monitor from the end table and turn it on so I can hear here if she does wake.

The fourth movie has just finished, and we're getting settled to watch the next one. This is what I need. A little of relaxation before shit gets real and I have to decorate the church and decide on hair and make up for us girls.

It doesn't take long for my eyes to drift shut with the sounds of Harry defending what is right in the background.

"Mama," a tiny voice pulls me from my sleep. I almost drop the baby monitor in my rush to get up. Except her voice didn't come from the monitor. She's standing against the coffee table waving the remote in her hand.

I glance to my left and right. Cami and Darcy are asleep. I guess the stresses of finals took its toll on all of us. "What are you doing in here? How did you get out of your crib?" I'm not sure why I bother asking. It's not like she's going to tell me.

"I brought her in here," Mom says from the entry way. "I woke her up when I got home so maybe she'll sleep for you tonight."

"Thanks, Mom." I point to my friends beside me. "I think we all fell asleep watching movies."

"It's okay. I'm happy to help." She smirks at me. "It seems like the only way I can is if I take it upon myself. You really need to learn to ask for help when you need it."

"I know, I know." I stand to grab Layla and swoop her into my arms. "How's my baby girl doing? You see your aunts over there sleeping?" Her tiny hands grip my shirt sleeves tighter as I twirl her around. "I think you should wake them up."

Setting her down, I turn back toward Mom. "What time is it?"

"Almost five."

"Shi-, I mean crap. We've got to go. Our fittings are in an hour." I start shaking Cami and Darcy awake. "Can you watch Layla while we go?"

"Sure thing."

"Guys, wake up. We need to head to the dress shop. We almost slept through our appointment."

"Let's go then," Cami mumbles. "But tonight, we are going to bed at a decent hour. I need sleep something fierce."

"You got it." We rush out the door to my car. I really hope this fitting goes better than the last. I don't know if I can handle disappointment today.

reaf

IT'S BEEN a few days since I've gotten to spend time with Tonya and I feel like I'm going through withdrawals. We've both been busy. Between work and studying for our midterms, there hasn't been a free moment to ourselves. When you think about it, it's a little ridiculous since we live twenty minutes from each other.

Will it always feel this way? Even when we live together? I can't imagine not missing her, but what if some of that infatuation dies when we're married. These are not thoughts I need to have while I'm under a truck, changing the oil. I need to be aware of my surroundings, and I'm not going to be able to do that if my thoughts keep heading in the direction of what ifs. I love her and that's all the matters. We'll work through any issues we encounter.

I turn around at the sound of my name, almost

running into the tire. See, this is what I mean by I need to be paying attention to my job. But that doesn't even matter because the person who called my name is the one, I'm going to make my wife in exactly one week.

She's standing at the edge of the garage, knowing she can't come in. Her long black hair lifts in the gentle wind. The only word to describe her is stunning. Even in in her baggy band t-shirt, tied up in a knot on one side, skinny jeans, and Converse, she takes my breath away. I don't know how I got so lucky, but I'm not going to do anything to screw it up.

"Hey, what are you doing here?" I duck out from under the truck I'm working on, and walk toward her. Toward my everything.

She plays with the ends of her hair. She's absolutely adorable when she's nervous. This is the first time she's ever came to my job without me asking her here. "Do you want to come to the house tonight and hang out with us?"

"Yes," I pull her into my arms and kiss her softly. "I want to be wherever you are. I've missed you."

I feel her relax into my body. "What's the matter?"

"Nothing," she answers. Taking a deep breath, she leans back. "Well, not exactly nothing. But it can be fixed."

"Is it something with your dress?" I know her and the girls went to a fitting last night. After her last one, this one surely couldn't have been that bad. But the way her body is wound so tightly, I know something is bothering her.

"No," she smiles. "My dress is fine. It's everyone else's dress that is crap." She pulls back from me completely. "They aren't even the right freaking color."

"Is it fixable?"

"It is, but we'll get them at the very last possible minute." She kicks a rock that's made its way onto the sidewalk. "I mean how hard is it to get the dress in the correct color. Hell, at this point I'd be happy with the girls wearing a little black dress. I know it's not traditional wedding attire, but trying to get these dresses out for everyone is exhausting."

"Is there anything I can do to help?" I hate that she's putting on this stress on herself without asking for help from anyone.

"Not really," she sighs. "Now it's just a waiting game and hoping they have the dresses in time. Maybe the girls and I can figure out some sort of backup just in case."

I smile even though it irks me that she isn't asking me to help her. I don't know the first thing about dresses or decorating, but I catch on to things pretty quickly. She keeps treating me like she can't lean on me when it matters. Maybe we should have eloped when she jokingly suggested it. She definitely wouldn't be as stressed as she is right now.

"Is the dress shop at least giving everyone a discount for getting the order completely wrong?"

"Yep. That's the silver lining to it. They are even throwing in Layla's dress for free."

The grin that sweeps over her face has me melting. At least that one less thing she has to worry about. Anything that makes her happy, makes me happy. "That's great."

I pull her closer to me, breathing her in. She smells like those soaps from that bath store, and coconut shampoo. I could stay like this forever.

"Reaf," my boss calls out from the garage. "You need to finish up this truck so we can get another car on the lift."

"I guess that's my signal to let you get back to work," Tonya mumbles into my chest.

"Yeah, I guess." My shoulders slump at the thought of her leaving, but I can't ask her to wait until I can clock out. She would be bored of out her mind, and I wouldn't be able to concentrate. Besides her friends are up from out of town, and they need some time together. Especially since she rarely gets to see them other than holidays.

"You'll get to see me tonight," Tonya whispers. "Go back to work and I'll go entertain my friends for a few more hours." She leans toward me as if to tell me a secret. "I love you, and I can't wait to call you my husband."

"I love you, too." I grin. "Now, get out of here so I can get back to work." I playfully swat at her ass, but miss by mere centimeters.

Walking back into the garage, I can't help but feel

giddy. She came to the shop to see me for something that could have been handled over a text message. That action has quelled my nerves about her missing me. I think we'll always have an opportunity to miss each other. Especially while we're both in school and the classes pull us in so many directions.

I don't let any of the shop shenanigans get in my way. I'm chipper, whistling while I work through oil change after oil change.

* * *

Cars line the road when I get to Tonya's house. This get together isn't as small as she planned. Unless…those cars are here for another house. But I recognize a few cars that I've seen here before.

There are a lot of voices that can be heard from where I stand on the porch. Are they having a block party? I knock, but nobody answers. They probably can't hear me. Instead of waiting around, I push the door open and walk inside.

The room is bursting with people. Family members that I met at the Burgess's New Year's celebration, and a quite a few that I don't recognize. The wedding is a week away, why is everyone here now?

"Reaf," Jason calls out from the crowd. "I was wondering when you were going to show up."

"Hello, sir." I glance around the room. "Did I miss a memo about a party, or something?" Surely something of this magnitude would have been mentioned before I got here. Tonya has been very detailed about the wedding planning. This isn't something that would have slipped her mind.

"We both must have missed it." He gestures toward everyone chatting. "Lucia's family came in a week early. Luckily they booked hotel rooms because we don't have anywhere for them to sleep."

"Why would they come early? It's not like there's anything to do in this little town." It's not a lie. The closest city is over thirty minutes away. They are going to be bored out of their minds.

Jason nods, grimly. "I have no idea. But Lucia and Tonya are going to be the ones playing host to them. I only hope it doesn't push Tonya overboard with all the stress she's been putting on herself."

"You've noticed it, too?"

"Yep. Maybe you can talk some sense into her. See if she'll pass some things off. I know she gave your sister some things to do, but it's not nearly enough. That child refuses to ask for help when it's needed."

"Do you know where I can find her?" I ask. "I'm sure she's not taking this sudden influx of people very well."

"Last time I saw her, she was heading to her room."

"Thanks."

He pats me on the back in solidarity. "Good luck."

I weave through everyone, muttering hellos and stopping to answer questions from those that I know. How in the hell do this many people fit in this house? It's not small by any means, but I know if this were a place of business, we'd be breaking fire code.

Finally, I make it to Tonya's room. It only took me twenty minutes to get from one side of the house to the other. I knock and wait for a response. When there isn't one, I know again, and call out her name.

"I'm hiding," she calls out. But moments later she's at the door opening it wider to let me in. Cami, Darcy, Charleigh, and Bianca are all sitting on Tonya's bed with two bowls of popcorn in the middle. The buttery scent hits my nose, and my stomach growls.

"Come in," she whispers. "Don't let them see that you're over here or they'll make me come out and socialize."

"I take it this," I point my thumb toward the room I just left. "Is a surprise to you, too."

"Do you think I would have invited everyone over to hang out if I knew over half my family was going to be here?" She scrunches her face so much her eyebrows are almost touching.

"Where are the guys?" I ask all the ladies on the bed.

Darcy is the first to reply. "Derrick is still on the road. I kind of hope they lose the next couple of games so he'll be here for the wedding."

I laugh. I can't help it. From the little bit of time I've spent with Derrick, I know he's living his dream. A loss would be a punch to the gut. Darcy's face falls. "I guess that's a little selfish of me. But dang it, I want him here with me."

Cami reaches over and rubs her back. "He'll be here. Even if he has to come in for the day and leave again. He won't miss it."

Darcy's responding smile is small, but the reassurance is enough for her.

Bianca is the one to answer. "They are in the far back corner of the yard. Hiding from everyone like we are."

"Why aren't y'all out there with them?" It's odd that they split off into groups.

"Because the popcorn is in here." Cami points to the bowls and grins. "And who wants to hang out with a bunch of guys talking sports anyway?"

Charleigh begins to raise her hand, but Bianca pushes it down. "What?" She asks, shooting a glare at her friend. "I happen to be following basketball this year."

Tonya grabs my hand and leads me to her bed, ignoring the bickering going on next to us. I gently squeeze her hand. "How are you holding up?"

"Okay, I guess." Her eyes are looking everywhere in the room but at me. I pull her attention to my face, and she sighs. "I thought the dresses being the wrong color was the worst that could happen. But then family started showing up while I was outside with our friends, and I don't know how I'm going to handle it. How am I supposed to finish the decorations, bouquets, and all of that while having to keep them occupied?"

Cami raises her hand as if she's still in school, "You could pass on some of the tasks to us." She waves her hand between herself and Darcy. "Hello, we're the wedding party. Our job is to make this as easy for you as possible."

Darcy gets up and rummages around Tonya's messy desk. I'm not sure how she finds anything on that thing with papers scattered all over the place. Finally, Darcy finds a spiral and a pen. Sitting in the office chair beside the desk, she opens up the spiral and looks pointedly at Tonya. "We're going to make a list of everything that needs to be done, and divide between us."

"Oh, shit," Cami mutters. "Darcy is in list making mode, run for the hills."

Darcy balls up a piece of paper, throwing it at her, and misses by feet. Cami is laughing so hard she almost falls off the bed.

Our friends' other halves come in, and we spend the rest of the night making lists and figuring out what needs to be done. I'm grateful for the friends we have, otherwise the workload would seem impossible.

When the house has quieted down, signaling her family's departure, we take our meeting to the kitchen. Lucia has left a full pan of brownies sitting on the counter for us. A note beside it reads, "Enjoy."

Tonya mutters something about her dress not fitting before she shoves a square of chocolate in her mouth. At least she seems calmer now.

tonya

I'M HIDING out in my room...again. Although my family is amazing, their presence is draining. The offers of help are also getting annoying. If I needed it, I would ask. Well, probably not. But still, they don't have to keep asking what I need done.

The list, and dividing of jobs, Darcy put together over the weekend helped immensely. We've gotten almost all the flower arrangements done, and are putting on the final touches. I'm going to need Darcy to show me her magical ways so I can keep my life in order. It would definitely help me better manage my time once Reaf and I are living together.

The thought has me terrified and excited at the same time. Is that even possible? I've never lived with anyone besides my parents and I don't even know *how* to run a household. And cooking is out of the question because I'm horrible at it.

My biggest worry is how is Layla going to handle it? I know she's only a year old, but this is the only home she's known. Will she act out when she doesn't get to see my parents every day? It's going to be an adjustment, that's for sure. I only hope we all get through it without getting frustrated.

"Tonya," Cami yells in my ear.

"What?" I snap back. Lifting my hand, I rub my earlobe. Son of a biscuit she's loud.

"Girl, I've been trying to get your attention for the past few minutes. Don't snap at me." She's wagging her finger in my face. She's going to make an awesome mom one day. I'll never tell her that, of course. She'd run for the hills and never look back.

"Sorry," I mutter. Grabbing the closest pillow on my bed, I place it in my lap worrying one of the corners. The sun is shining brightly through my sheer curtains, and I hate that I feel like I have to sequester myself to feel a bit of peace.

"What's the matter?" Darcy calls from the doorway, a plate of cookies balanced on her hand. The smell hits me, and I groan, knowing I can't have any even if I want them. I swear Mom is trying to keep me from fitting into that damn dress.

"Just thinking about what it's going to be like to have my own apartment, and how the hell I'm going to keep us all alive when I can't even cook."

Cami shrugs as if it's no big deal. "You can always order take out." She grabs a cookie from the plate and takes a big bite. "And I'm sure Reaf will cook for y'all," she mumbles around a mouthful of the dessert I want so badly.

"He said he would. But I feel like it's a responsibility we should both share." I place my fingertip on my lips. "I should take a cooking class, or at least watch some videos so I can make something simple until I find time to learn."

"That's a good idea," Darcy says as she places the cookies on my bed. Within reach. It's like they are trying to test my willpower. Cami knows how much I love my mom's baking, even if Darcy doesn't. That's another thing I'm going to miss. "And, I'm sure it's something he'll appreciate. Y'all could take one of those couples cooking classes. I know they have some in Dallas. It could be a fun date night."

Hmmm. I never thought of doing something like that. It would definitely be different than what we usually do, which is stay home and watch movies while Layla plays, or snuggles, with us. "I'll look into that. It would give us something to do before while we wait to have a honeymoon this summer."

"It sucks you can't go on a honeymoon right away like most people." Cami plops on the bed, and grabs another cookie.

The sweet, gooey, chocolatey temptation has pushed me past my limits and I take a cookie for myself. If I eat in small bites it doesn't count right? "I know. But this is the only time we could ensure everyone would make it to the wedding." I cringe when I see the pang of sadness hit Darcy. I know she's worried Derrick won't make it, but he'll be here. Travis accidentally let it slip to Reaf. He's going to surprise her, and I can't help but love how dedicated he is to her.

"At least you won't have to worry about classes when you go." A small smile forms as she changes the subject.

"That is true," I reply. "We aren't taking any summer classes. We're going to use those few months to enjoy being newlyweds."

Another cookie is calling my name, but instead of grabbing one, I push the plate to the other side of my bed. I won't eat them if they are over there, out of easy reach. At least that's what I tell myself.

"So, what's on the agenda for today?" I ask Darcy. She is the keep of the lists after all. Thank goodness she volunteered to handle that part, and I'm not the one keeping up with it.

She pulls her phone out of her back pocket and opens up an app. Scrolling past all the things we've already checked off, her finger stops on the main task we need to do today. "It looks like we need to go to the church and see where we're going to place the decorations and finalize a couple of details with the pastor."

"Hiding out in here isn't getting anything done. Let's head to the church." I stand up, grabbing my purse. "How much of my family is here right now?"

Darcy grabs the plate of cookies to return them to the

kitchen on our way out. "Just your great-grandmother, one of your aunts, and your mom. Why?"

"Just trying to figure out how many people I need to deflect on our way out the door."

As soon as we walk out of the room, I take a quick look inside Layla's room. She's still peacefully napping. Waking her up from her nap is the last thing I want to do.

Luckily, nobody else has shown up since Darcy joined us in my room. My mom, Tia Lisa, and Lala are all sitting at the table, coffee mugs in hand, talking. "Hey Mom." I make my rounds and hug everyone. "Can you keep an eye on Layla? We have to run to the church to finish some stuff up."

"Finally," she throws her hands in the air. "She asks for help." Smiling, she answers, "Of course, I'll watch her. You don't even have to ask. She's in capable hands between the three of us."

"That's what you think." I smirk. "You forget she's mobile now, and will get into *everything* in a blink of the eye."

"I raised you, didn't I?" One of her eyebrows quirks up. Damn, I wish I could master that. "I think we can manage."

"Okay. Have fun, but don't let her sleep for too much longer or she'll never go to bed tonight."

She ignores me and continues her conversation. "Well," I say to the girls. "Looks like it's time for us to go." This is one of the last big tasks we have to take of and then it should be smooth sailing.

* * *

"What do you mean we can't use the church?" My voice is almost a screech. I'm sure glass is breaking somewhere. "I'm getting married this weekend. How are we going to get married now?"

The lady on the other end of the phone is panicking. I can hear it in the small tremble in her voice. "I'm sorry, ma'am. But the church flooded over the weekend and we won't have the carpets replaced until early next week."

What am I supposed to do now? We don't have a backup plan. My family is huge and there's no way we can find something else on such short notice. The receptionist for the church is still talking but I don't hear a word she says. Instead, I pass the phone to Cami. She can deal with it. Because, right now...I can't. All this planning was for nothing. We're going to have to push the wedding back, and my family is going to be out all the money they spent to stay here for the week.

I thought it was odd when the doors to the church were locked. For as long as I can remember the doors have always been wide open. The sunlight hitting the stained-glass windows throwing color patterns on the floor. I should have known then that something was wrong. Maybe it's an omen, and we're rushing into this too soon. There's absolutely no way so much could go so wrong without it having a meaning.

Behind me, I hear Darcy say, "Thank you." They must have been on speaker phone so they wouldn't have to repeat everything.

Cami sits on the steps next to me, pulling me into an embrace. "It's going to be okay. We'll figure something out."

"How?" I croak. Tears are streaming down my face. When did I start crying? "I can't think of one place that will have availability for this weekend."

"You never know. Darcy and I will make some calls when we get back to the house. What do you say we stop by Brew's Clues, grab some coffee to refuel, and attack this problem with fresh eyes?"

My face is buried in my hands. "What's the point? It's not going to happen." Shaking my head, I look up at my best friend. "It's a sign. First my dress didn't fit, then the dresses for you and Darcy were completely wrong, and now this?" I wave my hand toward the church behind me. "It's not meant to be. At least, not right now. It's too soon for us."

Cami grabs my face until I'm looking directly into her eyes. "Hey, don't talk like that. You two are meant for each other. I've never seen a couple more in love or in sync with each other. Y'all are those ridiculous, sickly sweet couples that make other people cringe. But you *are* meant for each other. I don't want you to doubt that for a second."

I'm about to say something, but she's not done. "Give Darcy and me a chance to fix this. Don't let cold feet freak you out, and ruin a good thing."

I consider what she's saying, but fear gnaws at my insides, making me second guess everything. All the problems I've faced in the past week add up, and I have my doubts. In the end, I nod. "Okay, but if we don't have a solution by noon tomorrow, I'm calling it off."

Cami and Darcy both wince at my decision. "Okay." Cami squeezes me closer to her. "Just give us a little bit of time. We still have a few days to pull off a beautiful wedding that you and Reaf deserve. I swear to you, I will make it happen."

I don't argue with her. Once her mind is set on something, she does everything in her power to make it happen. I'll let her try, but I'm also going to be realistic.

reaf

WHAT IN THE world does "code red" mean? Travis text me those two words and I can't keep the feeling of dread from bubbling up inside me. I wish he would have elaborated, but he didn't. He also hasn't replied to the message I sent him fifteen minutes ago. Yep, whatever it is, it's definitely ominous. With over an hour left in my shift, there isn't much I can do about it right now.

Business has been slow at the shop now that most families are well into their Spring Break vacations. The only person consistently coming by is Jake's mom, Diane. The last time she walked in, my boss told her to leave or he would file harassment charges. She still drives by, but she doesn't stop anymore. This is becoming a problem, and I'm going to have to tell Tonya. I'm going to talk to Jake first. Maybe he can put a stop to it. I just wish I could understand why she's so adamant about stopping the wedding.

"I don't think the phone is going to magically ring if you stare at it." Rick's voice startles me. I almost drop said phone.

"You scared the crap out of me." I slide the phone into my back pocket. "I didn't even hear you open the door."

"That's because I'm very stealthy." He nods toward the phone I just shoved in my pocket. "What has you so focused on that thing?"

It's sort of odd that he's asking. We've never had any conversations like this. Mostly because he's my boss and I can't imagine opening up to him like that. But maybe an outsider's opinion would help. "Code red never means anything good, does it?"

He shakes his head. "Not in any circumstance I've ever been in. Why?"

That's about what I figured. My fingers massage the bridge of my nose. I can already feel a headache starting to form. What kind of catastrophe is happening now? "My buddy sent those words to me in a message, but he hasn't replied back. I have a feeling something else went wrong with my upcoming wedding."

Rick glances around the empty reception area. "Do you need to go home and see what it is?"

"I don't want to leave you in a bind," I reply. Being a burden is something I never want to do... In my work or personal life.

"Hold on," he puts his hand up in a stay gesture. "Is it okay if Reaf leaves early today?" He asks the empty room, and I shake my head at his antics. Even though we aren't close, I'm happy I work for someone with a sense of humor. "Really, though. Go home, take care of the crisis, and I'll see you tomorrow. We aren't going to have anyone else come in, and there's only one car on the lift. I've got it covered."

"Thank you, sir," my hand reaches out to shake his.

"No problem. If there's one thing I've learned in all of my years, it's that if the wife isn't happy, nobody is." He pats my back. "Now, get out of here."

I look at his left hand. There's no ring, and I'm wondering if he learned that the hard way. I don't take too long do dwell on it. Instead, I run back to the break room to grab my things and head to Tonya's house. If Travis isn't answering his phone after that message, it's almost a guarantee that everyone was called over there. I'm sure at Darcy's insistence. I wish she could have broken down everything for Tonya before this week. There's no doubt my fiancee's stress level wouldn't have gotten so out of hand.

Travis is standing on the front porch when I pull up to the curb with his phone in his hand. As soon as he sees me, he puts it in his pocket. "Dude, I thought you were never going to get here."

"I sent you a text asking what happened. You didn't respond," I argue.

"Sorry, man," he shrugs. "I was trying to help Cami. Tonya is in there losing her shit. The church had some sort of pipe burst and it flooded."

"Okay." Not fully understanding what he's trying to say, I reach past him to walk inside. But he grabs my arm.

"That means you can't get married there this weekend. The person they hired to replace the floors won't be there until early next week."

"Oh, shit." There are no other words. I knew whatever happened was going to be bad, but I didn't realize *how* bad. "How bad is it?"

He winces, not wanting to tell me. When I stare him down, he finally answers. "She's thinking about postponing the wedding."

That's worse than the church flooding. And without even saying anything to me. On that note, why wasn't I the first person she called about the church flooding? Walking around Travis, I push the door open.

He stops me once again. "Cami and Darcy have been calling around all day to find a new venue, but they haven't had much luck. Go easy on her. I think this is one of those last straw moments for her. I know we'll figure something out."

Go easy on her? She didn't even tell me we had a problem. Instead she shouldered it all by herself. How are we supposed to make a marriage work if we don't communicate? I mean I'm not going to go in there and raise hell, even if a part of me is disappointed she didn't turn to me. But I can't pretend that I'm okay with it either. "I know we will."

Travis closes the door behind us, and I walk toward the kitchen. It's where the raised voices are coming from. I can hear Cami trying to talk Tonya down. My girl looks defeated. As if she can't take one more piece of bad news.

She doesn't see me as I come in, having turned toward the glass door that faces the backyard. I wrap my arms around her waist, and whisper into her ear. "It's going to be okay. We'll find another place."

She turns around, stunned. Eyes, and mouth, wide open. "Reaf," she exclaims. "I-I thought you were at work."

"I was, but a little birdie told me I was needed here."

She rounds on Cami. "Did you call him?"

"No," Cami backs up. "I didn't call anyone except for the venues on my list."

Tonya's gaze cuts to Darcy. "It wasn't me."

Travis finally speaks up. "I texted him."

"Why?" Tonya whines. "I was handling it."

Travis steps closer to us. "No, you weren't. You were going to postpone it." He waves his hand toward me. "You didn't even tell him about what happened. You both need to decide on things. Just because the bride picks out most of the things doesn't mean you get to make all the final decisions. You both need to decide what's going to happen."

I've never seen Travis speak so passionately about something. But I also know where he's coming from.

Even though we were both raised without fathers, his mom wasn't much of a mom either. I respect him even more for sticking up for me.

"Thanks, Travis," I nod in his direction. "But I've got it from here." I gently turn Tonya until she's facing me. "I know there hasn't been any luck with the places y'all have called, but that doesn't mean we have to wait to get married."

"What do you mean?" She questions me. "If we don't have a place, *how* are we going to get married?"

My hand goes to her cheek, and I feel her body soften at the touch. "We do have a place." I point out the kitchen windows to the massive backyard.

"Are you serious? Do you have any idea how hard it's going to be to fit our families back there?"

Cami butts in. "Girl, we've done it before during the holidays. We can totally pull it off for your wedding."

Tonya turns her gaze back to me. "Are you sure?"

"We could get married in a dirty alley, and I wouldn't care. I'll marry you anywhere, as long as I get to be your husband."

The girls sigh a collective, "aw." Travis on the other hand mutters, "kiss ass" under his breath.

Tonya exhales. "Okay, a backyard wedding it is. We have 3 days to turn this place around."

Darcy is already busy making a list of things we need to do to turn the yard into something beautiful. "How many people can we get to help with yard maintenance and altering the decorations?"

"My mom was planning on taking the rest of the week off to help wherever we need her," I supply. "The shop has been slow so I'm sure Rick would let me take off."

"Great," Darcy chirps. "Let's do this thing."

By the time everything is planned out, I'm exhausted. I'm happy that we found a solution. Even still, there's a small part in the back of my head that wonders if I can be the husband Tonya needs, especially since she didn't even want to tell me what was going through her mind. We definitely need to talk...and soon.

IN TWO DAYS, I'll be married. The nerves that crept up before are nothing compared to what I'm feeling now. A part of me still wonders if it's too soon. If we need to date longer. But the bigger part is excited to see where my journey with Reaf takes us. Planning this wedding has definitely taken its toll on me, and our relationship. I haven't handled the stress very well, and tried to make important decisions without the one person I'm supposed to rely on. It's new territory for me, though. My parents and Cami are the people I've gone to for so long, and it's weird not to turn to them first. I'll do better. I have to.

The sun is shining through the kitchen window, and I watch a crew of guys working on the final touches in the yard. Mom hired a landscaping company to make the front and back yard pretty. There are bright flowers lining the sidewalk leading up to the door, and small bushes planted along the fence. One either side of the gate that leads to the backyard are two big rose bushes. Not all of them have bloomed yet, but I'm completely okay with that. Already this backyard wedding is shaping up to be more than I could have imagined, and I'm happy Reaf suggested it. We could have saved a lot time, money, and stress if we would have gone this route from the beginning. I'm kicking myself for not thinking of it.

"Whatcha doing?" Cami sidles up beside me while Darcy comes to stand on the other side.

"Just admiring the view. Hoping we can pull this off without a hitch."

"Bad things come in threes," Darcy says. "And, we've already had three issues happen. I think we're good."

"We also don't have to worry about forgetting anything the day of the wedding because everything will be here." Cami elbows me in the ribs.

I grab my side. "Ow. Why did you do that? Are you trying to bruise me up before my wedding?"

"Stop being a drama queen," she stares me down. "You aren't allowed to have any more meltdowns for the rest of the year. Especially after the one you had the other day. You should have a little more faith in your friends... And Reaf."

"What's that supposed to mean?"

"You didn't even tell him about the church. I know you're used to shouldering it all by yourself, but you have a partner in life, now. You have to learn to share those burdens."

"I know. I've been used to you being my partner in crime. Even when you're away at school."

She turns me toward her, and places her hands on my shoulder. "I'll always be here for you, no matter what. But it's time to start relying on your future husband. I have no doubt I'm leaving you in capable hands."

Tears begin welling in my eyes, as she pulls me into a hug. Darcy puts her arms around me, too. We're one tiny group hug, and I couldn't be happier with the friends I have. They know exactly what to say to get me through whatever I'm feeling.

Cami is the first to pull back. "Now, enough of the emotional craziness. Instead of doing a bachelorette party, we're going to spend the day together doing all sorts of stuff. Now, go get ready. We have to swing by and pick up Caroline in an hour."

"We can't have an all-day party," I argue. "There's still so much that needs to be done."

"Calm down, Tonya." Darcy throws her arm around my shoulder. "Your mom and Maggie are taking care of the arch, and picking up the chairs, tables and everything else."

"Are you sure they don't need us?"

"Positive," Cami turns me toward my room. "Now, get your ass in the shower so we can get this show on the road."

* * *

"Where are you taking me?" They put me in the backseat, as if that will keep me from seeing out of the windows. There are days I wonder about Cami's thought process, and today is one of them.

"Don't you worry your pretty little head," she calls back. "Just sit back and enjoy the ride."

"I guess I should be happy you didn't blindfold me." There's no way I would have been able to hand that. I squirm even thinking about it.

Darcy snaps her fingers from the seat beside me. "I knew I was forgetting something."

"That's not even funny," I retort. "It would have been a good way to piss me off."

Caroline snorts from the front passenger seat. "Like I was going to let them do it. You've been so full of tension lately that any crazy antics would have made you snap."

She's not wrong. I've been trying so hard to make everything perfect that I haven't taken the time to enjoy the actual planning. Instead, I've been griping at the people I care about and making life harder than it should be. "Guys, I'm sorry if I've been a pain in the ass."

"It's definitely been more than *if*," Cami points out. "You've been a freaking nightmare. But," she sighs. "That's okay because you are the bride." She glances at her side mirror before merging into the next lane. "Honestly, I'd be worried if you didn't go all bridezilla at least once."

"That doesn't really make me feel any better," I mutter.

Cami hears me anyway. "When have I ever said anything to make you feel better?" Shrugging, she adds, "I've always been brutally honest. It's one of the things you love about me."

She's right, of course. My best friend has no problem setting me straight when I need it. I only wish I could think of a way to show her how much I truly appreciate her. She's always been my constant, and I'd be lying if I said I wasn't worried about how this change in my life is going to affect our relationship.

We ride in silence until Cami turns on her blinker to take an exit I immediately recognize. "Why are we going to the mall?"

"Because," Caroline says. "You can't get married without getting pampered, first. We're getting manicures and pedicures before we do anything else."

"As long as we also get one of those cinnamon pretzels, I don't care what we do." Knowing these girls have put a lot of thought into whatever else they have planned for me, warms my heart. I feel the first twinge of excitement in my chest.

"Whatever the bride wants, the bride gets." Cami says as we pull into a parking spot.

"Well, let's do this thing." We exit the car and the light Spring breeze lifts the ends of my long hair. Oh shit. In all the madness of the past two weeks, I completely forgot to set up a hair appointment. Dang it, how am I going to get into a salon on such short notice.

The girls stop when they notice I'm no longer following them. "What's wrong?" Darcy asks. She's always the concerned one, and I love her for it.

"My hair looks like hell, and I'm not going to be able to get it done before the wedding." I stomp. Yeah, I stomped, so what if I'm having a tantrum. I think it's completely called for. I can't seem to win for losing.

"Oh," she waves her hand at me like it's a nonissue. "We already took care of that. Cami told me who your stylist was weeks ago, and scheduled it for you."

I run and throw my arms around the both of them so hard I almost knock them down. Waving Caroline over to join in our impromptu group hug, I squeeze her just as hard. "What would I do without y'all?"

"Have shitty hair?" Cami mumbles. "Ow."

Darcy poked her in the side for her comment, and I can't stop the laugh from bubbling up. "Seriously, thank all of you for helping me so much the past two weeks. I would have called it all off if I didn't have you three on my side." A tear escapes my eye. "See, y'all made me cry." I quickly wipe it away, not wanting them to think I'm upset. "Now, let's go get our nails done and grab some pretzels."

You wouldn't think cutting off three inches of hair would make a difference in the weight, but it feels so much lighter, and looks healthier. We also added in a few highlights to naturally dark hair. I don't even remember the last time I've gotten them done. Since before I was pregnant with Layla, at least. I can't stop running my fingers through it.

"Girl, you look like you're in one of those shampoo commercials." Cami grabs my hand before it makes another pass through my locks. "And, it's weird. You should probably stop."

"Leave her alone," Darcy butts in. "She doesn't pamper herself often, let her enjoy it."

"I've never heard a truer statement," Caroline adds. "I have to make sure I schedule in time for myself, otherwise I'll forget. I devote so much of my time to David that I sometimes forget who I am."

I stop in my tracks, almost causing the people walking behind us to run into me. "That's one of my biggest fears. Not just with being a mom, but also being a wife. What if I lose myself to those roles? I don't want to forget who I am, or my dreams."

Caroline takes my hands in hers, ignoring the dirty looks we're getting from passersby for stopping in the middle of the walkway. "That's not going to happen. I know I'm probably not the best person to give you advise in this area since my own marriage failed miserably, but you and Reaf will do fine. You'll both be able to chase your passions. And... You have an amazing example of that in your parents."

"But," I begin to argue, but she cuts me off.

"Nope, there's not buts," she shakes her head driving the point home. "If I know the both of you like I think I do, I know that you strive to have the type of marriage your parents have. They each have their own interests, but they still make time for each other. It's not always easy, and marriage is a lot of work. But if there's anyone who can do it, it's you two. The most stubborn, hard-headed people I know."

"Hey," I protest. "I'm not either of those things." Instead of agreements, I only hear snorts from my two closest friends. Whatever, I like to think of those quali-ties as determined. Another group of people glare as they have to split up to go around us. "Okay, we're moving. Don't get all huffy." I clap my hands together. "What do y'all have planned next? Please tell me it involves food."

I'm not a huge drinker, but this is one of the few times I wish I could get a drink while out and about. We're at a restaurant, well, it's more of a bar but they serve food. People are playing pool on the tables scattered throughout the room. Random signs cover the walls with no rhyme or reason. It's like a huge jigsaw puzzle, and there is very little space between each one. There's a raised stage area along a short wall where a band is setting up their equipment. The energy buzzing through the room is palpable, and I want to be a part of that.

"Where did y'all even find this place?" It is a bit of a trek from our area, but so worth it. This place is nothing like the bar and grills we have.

"This is my contribution to bachelorette day," Caroline says. "I've come here a few times with friends. It can get rowdy, but the bands that typically play here are pretty good. I wanted to give you a new experience and take you out of your element."

"You've definitely managed to do that." I eye the bag Cami brought in with her. It's a plain gift bag, but it seemingly appeared out of nowhere. "What's that?" I point toward it.

"This," Cami declares. "Is your bachelorette garb. Don't worry, it's nothing crude." My horrified expression must have clued her in to how I feel about that. "I kept it classy, otherwise Darcy would have kicked my ass."

She pulls out a white sash with "bachelorette" written in pink, cursive sequins, and puts it over my head, situating it across my chest. Next out of the bag is a tiara, with flashing lights surrounding the word "bride." But, I'm not the only one donning the all the flashy items. They each have ball caps that read "bride tribe," and are wearing their own sashes with their role in my wedding written across them. At least I won't have to suffer the weird looks by myself. "Y'all really didn't have to do this."

"Yes, we did." Darcy is repositioning her hat so she

can actually see everything from beneath the bill. "We may not be old enough to drink or do anything crazy, not like we would anyway, but we can still have the same experiences others have."

Cami stops a woman making her way toward the restroom. "Can you get a few pictures of us?"

"Sure," she says, and grabs Cami's outstretched phone. We ham it up for the camera, taking serious photos, silly face pictures, and just enjoying our night. "Congratulations. I hope you have many years of happiness," the woman says before leaving the table.

The band begins to play and we abandon our table to get closer to the stage. The plus side of all the flashy things they make me wear is we have no problem moving our way to the front. Shouts of "congratulations" follow behind us. We start dancing to our own beat, laughing, and living in the moment. The band mostly plays cover songs, but I don't care. I'm having the time of my life. These three sure know how to show a girl a good time, and I'm happy I have them with me tonight, and by my side on one of the happiest days of my life.

It's almost one in the morning when we pull into my driveway. Cami is staying with Darcy tonight so they can pick up our dresses on the way over here in the morning, taking one more thing of the list of things that need to be done. We dropped Caroline off on the way home since we picked her up, and her car isn't here.

Travis's car is parked by the curb, and shockingly, so is Jake's. I knew they were having the bachelor party here since Bryce is still in high school and can't really get into some of the places they were thinking about going. But I'm surprised they invited Jake. Don't get me wrong, Jake and Reaf have a decent friendship since we're co-parenting Layla, but they don't hang out much outside of that. He must have stopped by to see our daughter, and was invited to stay.

Once we're out of the car, I stop the girls before we go in. "Thank y'all for an amazing day. I literally couldn't have gotten through the past two weeks without you. I love you."

"Aw," Cami sighs. "You know we have your back. This is going to be the best damn wedding ever."

"Yeah it is," Darcy says. "Thank you for letting us be a part of your special day."

"I wouldn't have it any other way."

Cami reaches for the door. "I'm going to go tell Travis bye before we head to Darcy's." She disappears into the house, Darcy close on her heels. I can't wait to see her face when she sees Derrick Saturday morning.

I close the door gently behind me, and walk to Layla's room. She's sleeping soundly in her bed, tiny snores breaking up the quiet night. I lean over the crib railing, and place a kiss on her forehead. She moves the tiniest bit and I worry that I've woken her up, but she settles right back down and continues snoring.

I need some water before I go to bed. I didn't drink at all tonight because of the whole age thing, but dancing wears a person out. There's no doubt my body will be hurting tomorrow, but right now I'm parched.

I'm a few feet from the kitchen, and stop when I hear voices coming from the room. "You have to do something about your mom, Jake."

"What is she doing now?" He sounds exasperated, and tired at the mere mention of the woman who wanted to pay me off.

"She came by the shop last week telling me to call off the wedding so that Tonya could wise up and marry you, the father of her child." Reaf's voice is frantic. "I ignored it because it's crazy talk, but it didn't end there. She came in a few more times until Rick threatened to file harassment charges. She still drives by every single day."

"She is insane," Jake replies. "Why can't she just give it up and focus on her charity work like she's done my entire life."

"I wouldn't have said anything, but it creeps me out. What if she tries to crash the wedding?"

"She won't. Jason and Lucia got a restraining order taken out against her. But I'll deal with it. Does Tonya know?"

"No. I didn't want to give her one more thing to stress about since she's been handling most of the wedding stuff by herself."

Why can't Diane leave us alone? She was controlling when Jake and I were dating, but this takes the cake. I don't give them a chance to discuss anything else. "Why didn't you tell me?"

"Shit," Reaf mutters. "Tonya, I was going-"

"Don't bother." I forget about the water I so desperately wanted, and run to my room locking the door behind me. How could he not tell me something so important? Something that could potentially cause a problem on *our* day?

reaf

THE NIGHT WAS GOING SO well. We cooked steaks, sat by the fire, and just hung out without a care in the world. I couldn't have planned anything better for my bachelor party. I'm also grateful to Travis for doing a party that my kid brother, Bryce, could attend. He wasn't too keen on coming in the first place, but changed his tune once we ate and started hanging out. But now... The night has gone to shit. I managed to piss Tonya off without even realizing it.

When she didn't show up with Cami and Darcy, I assumed she went to bed. Jake was about to leave and I wanted to talk to him about his mom. I didn't think that Tonya would hear any of it. I hoped to keep the whole thing from her. Now she's in her room, and I'm not sure if I should go after her or give her some space.

"I'm going to head out," Jake mumbles. "You might, uh, want to explain everything to Tonya before she starts thinking up a million reasons why this is a bad omen."

"Yeah, I'll go do that." I start to walk out of the kitchen but stop. "You're still good to watch Layla tomorrow while we get everything set up, right?"

"Yep. I'll be here bright and early." He pauses on his way out. "And, don't worry about my mom. I'll deal with her."

"Thanks," I sigh. "I guess I better go beg for forgiveness for keeping this secret."

"Good luck," Jake laughs, then he's out the door.

I trudge to Tonya's room, not looking forward to the ass chewing she's about to give me. It's my own fault, I know, but that doesn't make it any easier. This is something I should have told her about when it happened instead of trying to sweep it under the rug, hoping it wouldn't come to light. Secrets have a way of coming out, whether you want them to or not. Even if the reason for them is to spare the feelings of the person you love most.

Leaning against the door, I knock three times. No answer. It's what I expected, but the snub still stings. "Tonya, please open the door so we can talk."

"I don't want to talk right now, Reaf. Just go home." It sounds like she's halfway between her bed and the door. If I know her the way I think I do, she's at war with herself over the decision to open the door or not. We obviously know which option I'm hoping she will choose.

I slide down the door until I'm sitting on the floor. My head falls back until it gently rests against the door. "I'll talk to you through the door if I have to, but I'm not going to leave. Not until you let me explain what happened."

The soft squeaking of her desk chair rolling across the carpet makes me breathe a sigh of relief. For once, she isn't going to be stubborn and is going to hear me out. "Okay, explain to me why Jake knows about what the hell is going on before I do." She whisper yells, trying to keep her voice down, not wanting to wake up Layla.

Her tone of voice isn't very welcoming, but what did I expect? I'm just lucky she didn't slap me or run to her dad to make me leave. Anytime she feels like she can't control a problem, Jason is who she turns to first. "Where do you want me to start?"

"How about at the beginning? That's usually a good place."

So, I do. I tell her about how Diane snuck up on me that first day. She told me I needed to call the wedding off so that Tonya could marry her son, the way it was *supposed* to be. And, I tell her how Diane is pretty much stalking the shop, trying to put some kind of fear in me. Like that's going to work.

The door opens abruptly, and I fall backwards. Tonya leans over me, "Why didn't you tell me all of this was going on?"

I shrug, which is a lot harder to do lying down than

one would think. "I came over that day to see what you thought about it, but you were at your dress fitting."

Her hands are on her hips and she's glowering at me. But, something in her softens and she reaches her hand out to pull me up. Leading me to her bed, she pats the space next to her as she sits down. "You could've told me after that. You were still here when I got home."

She is not going to like what I say next. I run my fingers through my hair trying to find the words that are going to piss her off the least. "Well, I talked to your dad about it while I was waiting on you. He suggested not telling you because we didn't want to put any more stress on you."

I cringe in advance because I know her reaction isn't going to be good. She doesn't disappoint. "My dad knew," she shrieks. Then remembering her daughter is asleep, she lowers her voice. "You both knew and neither one of y'all thought I should know?"

"I wanted to tell you, I did, but you were already freaking out about the decorations and how everything was going to get done before the wedding. I didn't want to give you one more thing to lose your shit about."

That little bit of sympathy I saw from her five minutes ago... Yeah, that's gone. She's glaring at me as if I should figure out a way to go back in time and fix the entire situation. I don't say anything else because honestly, she's scaring me. Instead, I let her simmer in her anger. Like I said, she has every reason to be upset with me. I'm certain she is envisioning each and every way she can beat the crap out of me to let some of that frustration out. We both know she would never act on it, though.

Tonya takes a deep breath and then exhales. She does it three more times before her shoulders relax. Some of the severity leaves her gaze, and she finally speaks. "I appreciate what you and Dad were trying to do. Notice how I said *trying*." She gives me a stern look. The kind only a mother knows how to deliver. "Even though I am the last to know, I forgive you and Dad for withholding the information. Only because I know your hearts were in the right place." She smacks my arm with the back of her hand. "Though, if any shit like this happens again, you better tell me or I will have your ass."

"So," I ask uncertainly. "Are we okay?"

"Yes." She nods to emphasize her answer. "But I'm not playing. If you want me to rely on you more, and come to you first. You need to do the same."

"I will, I promise." I grab her hand and lace my fingers through hers. "I'm so sorry for keeping it from you. You have no idea how much I've worried myself over this whole thing."

` "Apology accepted. Besides, I'm sure it will all be handled before Saturday if Dad and Jake have anything to do with it." She leans into me, her mouth presses against mine, giving me a soft kiss that I immediately want to turn into more. Tonya pulls away before I can even wrap my arms around her. "Now go home and get some rest, we have a lot of work to do tomorrow."

That is not how I saw this kiss ending. I'll do as she says, though. Anything to make her life easier. "Goodnight. I'll see you in the morning." I kiss her on the forehead before making my way to her door.

"I love you," she whispers to my retreating back.

"I love you, too. Go to sleep."

That conversation could have gone a completely different way. A way that might have ended with no wedding. I'm just happy that my girl is level-headed, and can see that I wasn't trying to be malicious.

I call for Bryce, and we head home. We are going to have to bust ass in the morning to make this a perfect day for Tonya.

tonya

MY BODY IS sore and aching. Which is why I'm sprawled out across my bed letting everybody else take care of the final touches. Yesterday all hands were on deck to finish up the archway and arrange the chairs in rows across the backyard. We set the tables against the side of the house until they are needed after the ceremony. I have to say, we did a damn good job putting this wedding together after having to change the venue on such short notice.

Layla is pulling out every toy she owns from the toybox. I can't even find the energy get up and get ready, much less freak out about the mess she is making. The wedding begins in two hours, and a tiny part of me feels horrible for not being out there and helping our families set everything up.

I roll over and peek out of the window only to see Reaf and Travis carrying the arch to the back of the yard.

There's a roll of white fabric sitting front and center, waiting to be rolled out when it's time for me to walk toward my new future.

Tears form in my eyes, and slowly roll down my cheek. This whole wedding is something I never envisioned for myself. When I found out I was pregnant with Layla, I figured I would be single until she was grown. I could barely balance school and work in the beginning of my pregnancy. Then Reaf came along and changed everything. He was stubborn and went for what he wanted. And... he wanted *me*. I am beyond lucky to have him in my life.

A knock at my door pulls my attention away from the window, and forces me to get off of my bed. I ease the door open just a sliver to see who it is. When I notice my cousin, Amelia, standing on the other side, I throw the door open and wrap my arms around her. We used to be so close growing up and when we got into high school, we sort of drifted apart. I didn't realize how much I missed her until now.

"Cuz, loosen your grip. I can't breathe." She's patting me on the back with one hand, while the other is trying to push me back to give her some space.

"I didn't know you were going to be here." I feel like a kid on Christmas morning. Some of my best memories include her, and I'm happy she's here to celebrate this special day with me.

She takes a step back. "Well, I couldn't miss my

favorite cousin's wedding. What kind of a crappy person would I be if I didn't come?"

"Don't just stand in my doorway like some sort of creeper, come in." I turn around and pick Layla up, adjusting her on my hip. "Close the door because Mom is crazy serious about the whole bride not seeing the groom thing."

Amelia closes the door and walks closer until she is standing right in front of me. She grabs Little Bean's tiny hand and gently shakes it. "Hi, Layla. I know it's only been three months since I last saw you, but you've gotten so much bigger." Of course, she's talking in that ridiculous baby voice I loathe so much.

My cousin is making goofy faces, and Layla is giggling as if it's the funniest thing she's ever seen. All three of us sit on my bed so that me and Amelia can catch up. It's been too long since we have had any sort of girl talk, and she has changed so much since I last saw her. There is a new shyness that she didn't have before. I want to know what killed the exuberant person she used to be. She was the life of the party when we were younger, and now... Now, she folds into herself, like she's scared of anyone seeing her. I noticed it when she was here for New Year's, but it's even more apparent now. I miss the old Amelia.

Cami barges into the room. Doesn't bother knocking, or anything else. "Tonya, the wedding starts in an hour and a half. Why aren't you getting ready?" Her voice is high and demanding. "I want your butt in that chair, *now*."

My eyes go wide, and Amelia laughs. "Hey Cami," she says over her shoulder. "Long time no see."

"I saw you not that long ago," Cami rolls her eyes. "You are now on hair duty while I do her makeup."

"Um, okay." Amelia breathes out, and it sounds more like a question than agreement. "How do you want your hair, cuz?"

"I don't know. Ask drill sergeant, Cami over there."

Cami huffs in frustration. "You were always great at braids when we were kids, why don't you do french braids on the sides to meet up in the middle. Then, we can do loose curls for the unbraided hair."

"I can do that," Amelia replies. "I need a few hair ties and bobby pins."

Cami digs around in my drawers until she finds what she needs. After she gives the hair accessories to Amelia, she grabs my makeup and gets to work.

Darcy comes in a few moments later, and plays with Layla. Keeping her occupied until Cami and Amelia are done glamming me up. I didn't have this sort of treatment when I got ready for prom. It's maddening trying to follow both of their directions. My head is being tilted and turned so much that a headache begins to form.

I breathe a sigh of relief when they are done. Amelia helps Layla pick up her toys while I pull all of our dresses from the back of my closet. Next are our shoes. Each of us will be sporting a pair of Converses as we walk down the aisle. There's no point in being uncomfortable for the short amount of time we'll be standing in front of everyone.

Amelia is about to make her departure when someone knocks on the door. "Tonya," Reaf's voice floats through the air.

Crap. "Don't open it Amelia. If Mom finds out, she'll throw a fit."

"I'm not going to come in, weirdo." His husky laugh sends tingles throughout my body.

Butterflies erupt in my stomach, and I'm beginning to feel nauseated. Why are my nerves kicking in now? It's definitely *not* the time for that to happen. I lean against the door, wanting to know why he's here when he should be in Layla's room getting ready. "Do you need something?"

"No. I ju-," he stutters, nerves making his voice waver. "I just want to tell you that I love you, and I cannot wait to make you my wife. You mean everything to me, and this is the *best* day of my life."

"Stop, you're going to make me cry," I sniffle. "I love you, too. You should probably get ready; the ceremony will begin soon."

"Always so bossy," I hear through the door. "I guess I'll see you at the altar."

"There's no guessing. I'll see you there." A smile creeps onto my face. "Just remember, you signed up for this."

"And, I'd do it again if I had to."

This man, who wanted to date a pregnant girl, and has been there every step of the way for my daughter… He has me, heart and soul.

"Okay, Lover Boy," Cami yells. "Get away from the door before I have to redo all of Tonya's makeup."

"Yes ma'am." I'm sure he probably did a smart assed salute, and I wish I could see him right now. I'll wait because seeing him at the altar will be worth it.

"I guess it's time for me to get my ass dressed, too."

"Yep, but let us get dressed first so we can get you into your dress and get Layla ready last. Caroline was finishing one last thing up, and she'll be in here soon."

Amelia takes the opportunity to exit the room without a word. I'm definitely going to have to figure out what's going on with her.

The girls look amazing in their bridesmaids' dresses. Now that they are the right ones, at least. They each wear a turquoise skater dress with black Converse. Plus side, they won't be sweating while we're outside.

I, however, feel like I'm carrying another body on me. I love the dress, even though you can't see my turquoise shoes underneath all the tulle, I just didn't expect for it to weigh so much after I put it on. Layla looks like a tiny princess. Her dress is almost exactly like mine except for the small sparkles adorning the skirt in various places. She's wearing a crown of turquoise flowers on top of her head with ribbons curling behind her. This girl is going to be the showstopper.

Cami looks out the window to make sure everyone is where they are supposed to be. In less than twenty minutes I'll be walking toward the person I love. The one who will always be my home.

Mom sweeps in and immediately bursts into tears. "Mija, you look beautiful."

"Not you, too," Cami groans. "If you make her cry, I won't have enough time to fix her makeup."

"Oh hush," Mom chides. "Just wait until it's your turn. I'll be a blubbering mess then, too."

Cami's face scrunches up, and she pales. For someone in a committed relationship, I find it hilarious that marriage terrifies her.

"I wanted to give you these things before you walk into your new life. You already have something new and something blue." She points to my dress and my shoes. "This necklace has been passed down from mother to daughter in our family. Lala gave it to me, and I'm giving it to you." It's a gold chain with a small, simple cross suspended from it. Mom stands behind me, pushes my hair to the side, and fastens the clasp before letting my hair fall back into place.

She taps her chin. "Now, for something borrowed." She places the small white handkerchief she had clenched in her hand. "I want this back after the wedding."

"Even if it's all wet and snotty?"

"Even then," she replies. "Reaf is already out there waiting for you. I'll head out there so you girls can come out of this room. I'm sure you're sick of being in here."

"Thank you, Mom." I pull her into a hug. And, if I hold for her longer than intended, who cares? After today, I'll be in a home. One where I won't see her every day, and the thought still scares me, but I know she'll be there for me whenever I need her.

"You're welcome. I'll see you girls out there."

Minutes pass before we walk out of my room. I'd be lying if I said I wasn't relieved to be out of those four walls. It was almost claustrophobic. It doesn't take long before Darcy's squeal reverberates off the living room walls.

"Surprise," I yell, happy that I was able to help keep this secret.

Derrick is standing next to Travis and Bryce, with a sobbing Darcy in his arms. The three of them are in simple black tuxes, and wearing turquoise bow ties. They all look so dapper, and I can't wait to see my man in a few minutes.

"You knew he was coming?" Darcy screeches.

"Well, duh." Cami shakes her head. "He's wearing the tux, isn't he?"

I jab her in the side. "Stop being a jerk. She hasn't seen him in two weeks, cut the girl some slack."

"Fine," she mutters.

Dad walks out of the kitchen, eyes glistening in the

sun filtering through the windows. Shit, if he cries, I'm going to lose it. "Is everyone ready?"

A chorus of "yeses" ring through the room. Everyone lines up in the kitchen. Darcy with Derrick, Caroline with Bryce, and Cami with Travis. Layla holds onto to Cami's hand. I have no idea how she's going to make it all the way down the aisle, but I have no doubt that it will be the most adorable thing ever. I just hope somebody gets it on video.

Dad comes to stand beside me. "Are *you* ready?"

I nod, and throw my arms around him. "Yes, Daddy. Thank you for everything. I wouldn't be the person I am, or standing here today about to marry my soulmate, without your love and guidance."

"I love you, baby girl. You make your old man proud. I know I was leery of Reaf at first, but I know that he'll do everything in his power to make you happy."

"That's all a girl ever really wants."

My friends start filing out of the kitchen, and we make our way toward the back door. I glimpse Layla toddling her way behind Cami, smiling and clapping. My heart warms instantly.

"Let's do this," Dad whispers. His voice is tight, trying to keep a leash on the tears I know are threatening to fall.

My right foot crosses over the threshold, and I take my first step on my next adventure.

TEN

reaf

BIRDS ARE FLITTING through the air, chirping back and forth to each other. The sun is shining brightly in the sky, and a gentle breeze rustles the leaves of the few trees in the backyard. Me, I'm standing beneath the arch counting down the minutes until my bride joins me.

I thought I was a sweaty, awful mess when I proposed to her, but that was nothing compared to how I feel now. What if she changes her mind? Even though she assured me she would see me at the altar, I can't keep the thought from popping up in my mind. I shouldn't dwell on it, but until we are both standing up here, in front of our families, doubt is going to be there.

Sweat gathers along my hairline and begins rolling down my neck. Our families are sitting in the chairs smiling up at me. We didn't bother separating them today with a bride and groom side, and I'm happy to see everyone mingling and getting along.

My hands keep creeping up, of their own volition, to readjust my bowtie. I have never been one to fidget, but the anticipation is getting the best of me. Mom catches my attention when she lifts up her hand. She mouths "stop" and gives me a reassuring smile.

Somebody, I'm not sure who, begins playing some instrumental song from a bluetooth speaker, and my heart begins racing. It's time. Darcy and Derrick walk out onto the fabric runner leading from the back door to where I stand. Darcy is absolutely beaming. She must have liked our surprise, and I'm happy that she can be with the one she loves on mine and Tonya's special day.

Caroline and Bryce are next. He looks like he'd rather be anywhere but here. Caroline whispers something into his ear, and he laughs with a snort. His cheeks redden. It obviously doesn't take much to make my little brother blush. Now I want to know what she said. Cami and Travis walk out, hand in hand rather than have their arms looped together. They look like they are taking a walk in the park instead of walking down the aisle in a wedding. I have a feeling that was Cami's doing. She's such a commitment-phobe. I'm honestly shocked she's in a relationship.

Sweet little Layla follows behind Cami and Travis. She toddles down the aisle, and when she sees me, she runs as fast as her little legs will allow. "Weaf," she yells, getting a chuckle from everyone in attendance. She finally makes it to me and I sweep her up in my arms. She grabs my face with both hands and gives me a big kiss on the lips. I love this girl as much as I love her mom. They make my life better, and I can't imagine a day where I don't get to see them.

The music changes to the wedding march and our guests stand, waiting for Tonya to make her appearance. She doesn't immediately step out of the house, and my heart almost beats out of my chest in fear. She's bailing on me... on us.

Finally, the door opens wider, and my heart stops. Tonya's arm is looped through her father's and she is the most beautiful person I've ever seen. I mean, she's beautiful every day. But today... She looks like *royalty*. Her dress is strapless and fitted to show off her figure. One thing is for sure, my girl has curves in all the right places, and I can't wait to strip her out of her dress when we get home tonight. A full tulle skirt begins at her hips and is so long it brushes the ground. I can see a sliver of her turquoise Converse as she walks down the aisle toward me.

Layla claps excitedly in my arms. "Mama." She's reaching for her as they come closer to us. A smile so bright it rivals the sun is plastered on Tonya's face. I can't believe I doubted she would walk through that door. She's my forever, and I'm hers. It's something I've known from the first time I laid eyes on her. She irritated me, yes, but I couldn't deny the pull I felt toward her. It's even stronger today.

Jason and Tonya stop a mere foot before me, and it takes everything in me not to reach out to her. Not to pull her into my arms and never let her go. Jason turns to his daughter and lifts the veil over her face until it rests against her hair. After giving her a kiss on the cheek, he turns to me. Holding his hand out, he waits until I take it before shaking. "Be good to my baby girl." A tear slips down his cheek, and he takes Layla from my arms to sit with them.

"Yes, sir," I reply. "For as long as I'm breathing, my world will revolve around Tonya and Layla."

Nodding, he turns and takes his seat next to Lucia. Tonya steps forward until she's directly in front of me. "Hi," she whispers.

"You look like a princess," I say without thinking. Where the hell did that come from? The tips of my ears burn, and I'm pretty sure my face is a bright shade of red. "I mean, hi back."

She giggles, and opens her mouth to say something else, but our conversation is cut short. The pastor speaks loudly to be heard by those sitting in the back rows. "We're gathered here today to join Tonya and Reaf in marriage."

I drown out whatever he is saying, and stare in awe at the woman in front of me. How in the world did I get so lucky? Out of all the guys she could have dated, and fallen for, she chose me. She said yes to my awkward proposal. I will do everything in my power to be the husband she deserves.

"Reaf," Tonya whispers.

"Huh?"

"You need to repeat the vows."

"Oh, yeah. Sorry, I couldn't stop admiring you."

"I wish I could kiss you right now"

"Who says you can't?" I smirk and wink at her.

"Can we get on with the ceremony?" The pastor leans in to get our attention. "If the both of you focus, I can do this quickly, and you can continue your conversation."

The both of us nod emphatically, and the rest of the ceremony goes by without a hitch. The part I've been looking forward to all day is finally here. "You may now kiss your bride."

I pull Tonya toward me without hesitating. A piece of hair has fallen from her braid, and I sweep it back behind her ear. Placing my hands on either side of her face, I lower my head until my forehead is pressed against hers. "Will you kiss me already," she demands.

Nothing else needs to be said. My mouth meets hers, and there are explosions. I pull her closer to draw out the kiss as she throws her arms around my neck. I spin her into a dip, and let my mouth makes promises of our life together. Our families cheer and clap, but it's all background noise. My focus is one hundred percent on my wife, and I let that fact swirl around in my head before lifting her back up and pulling back. If I keep kissing her like that, we'll have to leave the wedding before the party has even started.

"Let me introduce you to Mr. and Mrs. Harrington," the pastor announces over the cheering people in the yard.

"Are you ready to party, Mrs. Harrington?"

"You better believe it, Mr. Harrington." She throws her arms around me and kisses me one more time, laughter filling our ears.

We don't bother letting our bridal party walk in front of us, I grab her hand, twirling her once, before running down the aisle. This is a moment I will cherish for the rest of my days, and I can't wait to get started on our journey together.

epilogue

THE RECEPTION IS in full swing, and this dress is stupid heavy. I wanted to change after our first dance, but Reaf insisted I keep it on. His exact words were "I want to peel every layer of that dress off of you as soon we close the door behind us." Who am I to argue with that logic?

One of the kegs my parents bought is already gone, and the food is running low. These are the parties I miss from my childhood. I'm betting most of my family will crash here tonight, wherever they can find space. I'm drinking a glass of punch with a napkin under my chin trying to save my dress from any spills. Amelia steps next to me. She wraps an arm around my shoulder, making me jostle my drink. I hold my hand away from my body, if this is going to spill, it's going to do happen on the grass and *not* my dress. "Your wedding was beautiful, Cuz. You've definitely found yourself a keeper."

"Thank you." My arm goes around her waist, pulling her in for a side hug. "When will I get to see you again? I don't want to go months without speaking to you."

"Next weekend," she replies flippantly.

"What do you mean next week? Did you find an apartment in the area?"

She clears her throat and looks everywhere in the room, except at me. "Well... Funny story. Things haven't been too great back home. Rumors are flying and people are being down right assholes. I can't deal with their nonsense anymore." She takes a deep breath. "Since you're moving in with Reaf, I asked your parents if I can stay with them until I get on my feet."

"Oh. My. Gosh. I'll get to see you almost every day." I'm jumping as much as my dress will let me. Details of what happened to make her run are needed, but not tonight. My heart breaks for her and I don't know what to do to fix it. "Are you going to go to school?"

"I'm going to take the year off. I need to find myself, my passions, and anything else I can find to help me find myself." Her arms are wrapped around her stomach, trying to keep me from *seeing* her.

"I can help you find a job, if you need any help."

"Thanks, I really appreciate it." She nods toward the space sectioned off for the dance area. "Your friends haven't gotten off the dance floor all night."

"Well, you know Cami. If she has an opportunity to dance without abandon, she's going to do it."

"What about the other two?"

"They haven't seen each other in a couple for weeks. I think they are making up for lost time."

"You have a great group of friends here."

"They'll be *your* friends, too. If you let them."

Amelia is about to say something, but Cami chooses that moment to get off the dance floor, and right in my face. "They are ready for you to throw the bouquet."

"Okay. Let's do this thing."

My uncle's voice booms across the backyard. "I need all the ladies that aren't married to form a circle in the middle."

Once everyone is in place, I turn around and close my eyes. I know there is some superstition about catching the bouquet, but I want anyone who catches it to find some sort of happiness. Even if it's only looking at the flowers and thinking they're pretty.

"On the count of three," my uncle bellows. "One. Two. THREE."

I lift my arms up and the bundle of flowers leave my hands. There's a shuffling of feet behind me, all the ladies doing their best to grab them out of the air. I turn just in time to see the bouquet land in Cami's hands. She wasn't even trying to catch them. Her eyes widen in fear as she looks from me to the bouquet. She calmly walks to the table to set it down next to the speaker. She picks up a tired, and cranky, Layla and starts dancing, like nothing happened. As if she didn't just have a freak out moment. My best friend is so weird. I shake my head and join two of the most important girls in my life.

The afternoon turned to evening, and it's starting to get late.

Moments later, Reaf's arms wrap around my waist and he sways to the music with me. Leaning down he whispers in my ear, "Ready to get out of here?"

I look back at him and see longing in his eyes. He's ready to spend our first night together as husband and wife, and I can't deny I'm eager as well. I nod and point to my mom.

"Mom," I say. "We're about to head out. You're okay with watching Layla, right?"

"Yes," she assures me. "Get out of here and have fun."

"But not too much fun," Dad mumbles. I laugh, guessing I'll always be his baby girl. Even when I'm about to step out on my own path.

"I love y'all. Thank you for helping me make this happen."

"We would do anything for you." Mom pulls me in for a quick hug. "Make sure you tell everyone goodbye before you leave."

Of course, I'm going to tell my family bye. They took time out of their busy lives to help me celebrate this amazing day.

As I'm making my farewells, I can't help but notice the way Randall keeps glancing at Amelia. I'm not sure how I feel about that, but I don't have time to think about it. Reaf has my hand in his and he's pulling me toward the side gate. Not only is this our first night married, it's also the first night we'll be spending in our apartment. I can't help but wonder how different it's going to be when it's just us. I'll have time to figure that out later. Right now, all that matters is ending this night in the arms of the man I love.

The drive doesn't take long, and I think he was speeding for part of it. Not that I blame him. We find a space right in front of our building, and Reaf hurries to turn off the ignition. He rounds the car and opens the door for me. We run up the stairs until we are in front of our door. He puts the key in the lock, and turns it until the deadbolt releases. He does the same for the door-knob, and swings the door open.

Before I have a chance to take step, he bends down and lifts me into his arms. Turning sideways, he crosses the threshold. But he doesn't stop there. He kicks the door closed behind us, and continues into our bedroom. It's still undecorated. I contemplate bringing my Bush posters with me when I get my things, but I'll leave those for my cousin.

He sets me down on the edge of the bed, and takes a step back. "You are stunning."

Blushing, I lean back. "Thank you."

He pulls me up and begins taking all the pins out of my hair. He bends down and slides my shoes off of my feet before standing back up. His touch is tender as he traces the line of my collarbone, and I can't stop shivers from taking over my body. He looks for the clasps that will loosen my skirt and when he can't find them, I point them out. He shifts until he is behind me and begins unbuttoning my bodice. I can only watch his reflection in the mirror of our dresser. Once he has the last one undone, the dress falls to the floor. The both of us stare into the mirror, watching each other's expressions. Mine is full of wonder and awe at the man I'll spend the rest of my life with. His... he has heat and desire in his eyes.

Reaf helps me step out of the puddle my dress has made and lowers me onto the bed until he's hovering over me. "I love you, Tonya, with all my heart and soul. I plan on spending the rest of the night showing you just how much."

"I love you, too." My voice is soft whisper into the quiet room. "Let's begin our life together."

Prologue

Couples are spinning around the floor, celebrating the marriage of the girl I used to have a crush on in high school. But she isn't the one capturing my attention. No, it's the girl I haven't seen in years.

Amelia, Tonya's cousin, used to spend the summers here when we were kids. She was so full of life, and always bouncing around like a damn cartoon princess. She saw the world through rose colored glasses while I saw it for the shit hole it actually is.

Something has changed, though. Her smile is forced when people talk to her. Her gaze barely moving from the floor unless someone is directly in front of her. I've wondered about Amelia since seeing her at the New Year's party at Tonya's. The weight of the world on her shoulders was evident then, but it's worse now. As if she's one straw from breaking into pieces.

I know that feeling all to well. Growing up the way I have, it's hard not to be cynical. Seeing all of my friends coupling up and living their happily ever afters pushes me further toward the fringes. But maybe I can befriend Amelia and we can be in our own little world of misery.

Someone slaps me on the shoulder. "Dude, you should smile more." Marshall laughs from beside me. He's always so upbeat about life. I envy him. He's never had to struggle. At least, not the way I have. The only time I've seen him mope is when Bianca wouldn't answer his calls last year. Now that he has his tattooed vixen by his side, he walks around as if nothing could burst his happy little bubble. I wonder what it's like to be that excited.

I shoot him a wide grin. "Is this better?" My lips straighten out as the music changes to one of those line dance songs that are customary at weddings.

"That might be the fakest smile I've ever seen." Shaking his head, he directs his gaze to the group of girls dragging a protesting Tonya toward middle of the yard where everyone is dancing. "It's a time for celebration." Noticing my scowl, Marshall's brows pinch in worry. "You're not still harboring a crush on Tonya, are you? I thought you said you were over that when you got in that fight with Jake last summer."

"No, I'm not interested in her anymore," I roll my eyes. "I haven't been since before we graduated." Crossing my arms over my chest, I take in the scene. Christmas lights are strung throughout the trees and a couple of floodlights illuminate the yard. We're all dressed in our Sunday best after a last minute hitch forced the wedding to be moved here. "I just don't want to be here."

"Being here is better than being at home," Marshall gives me a knowing glance. Yep, my home life sucks. But this sucks just as much.

He's not going to leave me alone about this. He's determined to make everyone as deliriously happy as he is. "I'll try to have a good time." Bianca moving closer to us catches my eye. "I think your girl is looking for you."

"So she is." He turns until he's standing directly in front of me. "For real, Randall. Have a good time. Be happy for them." He doesn't wait for a response. Instead, he jogs toward Bianca and wraps his arm around her waist. Lifting her up, he twirls her around until her head falls back in laughter.

Jealousy swirls through my gut. I may be bitter about love and relationships, but I *want* that. I want someone that gets me on a deeper level than anyone else.

Amelia stands and my eyes focus on her once again. Sadness surrounds her and I want to know who put it there. Not knowing if I'll ever see her again, I take a step in her direction. Before I make it over to her, Tonya's hooked her arm around her and sweeping her off to the house.

My shoulders sag, and I turn toward the side gate, ready to leave the party. Passing by the windows, I can't help but glance at the two women standing there. Amelia's wrapped in Tonya's embrace. I want nothing more than to walk inside and comfort her. Something draws me to her, and I can't explain it.

Fighting the urge to open the door, I continue toward the gate knowing I'll never get the chance to know the girl who seems just as broken as I am.

acknowledgments

This book was so much fun to write. It gave me a chance to write Tonya and Reaf's happily ever after. The process is never an easy one.

Thank you to my cover designer, KP Designs, and my editor, Shelly, at Small Edits. I couldn't do this whole thing without y'all.

I also want to thank my Alpha readers. You find my mistakes and help me make my words stronger. Seriously, you gals rock!

To my tribe, Kelsie and Tasha, I don't know how I would do life without y'all. I'm lucky to have the two of you on my side. And, Aurora, you are the only reason I get shit done. Thank you for helping keep me in line.

Nessa, my sista from another mista, thank you for being you. For always being in my corner and cheering me on.

Hubs, Boy Child, and Wee One, you are my reason for breathing. The inspiration on the hard days, and the people that make me laugh the most. I love you.

Mom and Dad, I love you, and your support means EVERYTHING!

Dreamers, thank you for being an awesome group to

hang out in. Y'all give me so many ideas, and I don't know that I'll ever be able to use them all. Y'all are the real MVPs.

Readers and bloggers, thank you for taking a chance on a new author. Without you, my books would be sitting alone on my computer.

Silverwood Bulldog Series

Baseball & Broadway